Loyal to His Lies

Loyal to His Lies

T. C. Littles

www.urbanbooks.net

Urban Books, LLC
300 Farmingdale Road, N.Y.-Route 109
Farmingdale, NY 11735

Loyal to His Lies Copyright © 2018 T. C. Littles

ISBN 13: 978-1-62286-696-0
ISBN 10: 1-62286-696-7

First Trade Paperback Printing July 2018
Printed in the United States of America

10 9 8 7 6 5 4 3 2 1

Distributed by Kensington Publishing Corp.
Submit Orders to:
Customer Service
400 Hahn Road
Westminster, MD 21157-4627
Phone: 1-800-733-3000
Fax: 1-800-659-2436

Dedications

If you've ever been fucked over by love and wanted revenge, this story is for you.

If you've ever been manipulated by a man, caught in his whirlwind of lies and deception, this story is for you.

If you've ever been labeled as a "crazy baby momma" when he's still low-key thirsty, this story is for you.

Loyal to His Lies is dedicated to my ladies who wanna go hard but for one reason or another can't! No one is worth your peace of mind. With or without his help, raise your child and keep it moving. Trust, karma is a bitch, and fat meat is greasy.

And for my fellas who can relate, enjoy!

Acknowledgments

In life, I've learned to deal with trials and tribulations as they come. Many say I know how to make the best out of a crappy situation. Some have said I go through things to help others that will walk it after me. Whatever the case, I'm thankful to have opportunities. I'm blessed to have strength, endurance, and courage. I'm overly grateful to have:

Jayden, my son, I love you. I'm proud of you. You're amazing. You're smart. You're courageous. You face the world with your gorgeous eyes, never letting them see you sweat! To me you are everything, and I want the absolute best for you. Keep doing what you do, son. You've got it!

My beautiful daughter, Ella Janaé, beans, the world will be yours. You are beautiful, smart, determined, and the answer to many of my prayers. I want you to be your brother's keeper as he is yours. I love the both of you with all of my heart.

Rick Morrison, my husband. I love you. I value our bond. I've never met a man so loyal, caring, non-judgmental, and accepting. I consider myself lucky to have you in my corner and filling a void Jayden will not know of. **Anthony,** in time you will grow, mature, and understand. Until then, I will try to fill that void and help you along your journey. You are smart, and you are loved.

Big Ella (my grandma) and Michelle, my tag team duo. I love you as grandmother and mother. You both have made me the strong woman I am today. Because of you two, I can endure. I am able to overcome. I am able to take life's ass whippings with a grim expression and tricks up my sleeve. I'm blessed to have you guys in my corner and Jayden's support system.

My Autism community and those suffering with Lupus and other chronic illnesses, keep fighting. You are all warriors!

YEAH, I KNOW . . .

My childhood bio will not bring a tear to your eye. Unlike many of the crack-addicted babies born inside of the general hospital of my city, my pops drove me home in his brand spanking new 1982 Grand Prix to a house full of newborn clothes and every baby toy the department store sold. From day one of my existence, I have been placed on a pedestal and offered the most lavish items Detroit city had to offer. While other mothers saw their children as burdens or an increase in welfare stamps, my mom branded me a representation of her, which is to say, a mini player and a diva. I was spoiled rotten and adored; which is why I feel like the world should kiss my ass.

Growing up in the hood was a cakewalk for me. Unfortunately, not many kids can tell the same tale. I was not raised on government assistance, forced to save or scramble for my friend's leftover soda pop cans for deposits, nor did the light and gas company dig up our front yard, leaving us in the freezing cold without services because of nonpayment.

Back in the day, my pops was deep into the streets as a hustler. He pushed everything from dope to bootleg videocassettes of movies that were playing in the theaters. There was nothing like bragging to all of my friends that I was going to see every new release and rated R movie on the very first day. They either could not afford to go, or they were not allowed to go. I, however, got to skip school and go first thing in the morning so my dad could get the bootleg copies going early. I'd be right beside him, on the lookout for theater workers, while he taped the entire movie.

While he'd be out slanging copies on the corners and taking my momma to all the hair salons to get them off, I'd be charging those same friends of mine a dollar to watch the movie while I made the bootleg cassettes. My job was to change the blank VHS cassettes when the movie ended and then label it. I only hated doing this when there was a super live game of tag or hide-and-go-seek going on outside.

When life was good for my family, it was good and we shined. But when it was bad and my dad's hustles fell off, my mom kept her fronts up and held the family up effortlessly. The world never knew and will probably never know how tight shit got for us. "Play the cards you are dealt, Zaria. Fuck letting a nigga see you sweat," she stayed advising me.

My family was big on personas and having mutha-fuckas green with envy and jealousy. As long as I was under their reins, I was invincible to the bullshit and dreams Motor City hustlers sold their women.

By the time I turned eighteen, the world was my oyster and the hood was my playground. You could not tell me shit, even if you tried. Not even my mother and father could keep me in check. I was reckless with a capital R. Every shorty in the city wanted to be like me, and every hustler they were fuckin' with had his eyes on me. I stayed in fresh clothes, fly shoes, and gold jewelry. My head was heavy from rocking a queen's ego.

Well, unfortunately, there are two sides to every coin, and all good things eventually come to an end. In my case, they came to a screeching halt. Even with all the knowledge my moms made sure I was privileged with, I managed to break the cardinal rule and her chief motto, which was to not become a part of the common-folk crowd. She did not want me hanging around anyone that was foolish, basic, or uncouth. I was her polished daughter that she'd placed on a pedestal, and because of that, no one was good enough to run around with me. The females were too fast-tail and hot in the ass, and the dudes weren't much but corner boy hustlers.

It's funny when I think back on it because right out of the gate, Nardo was not about shit. But he was tearing my pussy out the frame, knocking the wires in my brain loose. All the wisdom I had been schooled with was flushed down the toilet with our first used condom, and I'd become more than common. Not only was I no longer a made bitch, but I'd disgraced my bloodline in the process. No one adores the fool, and unfortunately, knowledge costs. And boy, was I paying the ultimate price.

Well, where do I start? Every unwed mother has a woe-is-me story to tell, and there is nothing special about mine. Being a let-down to my parents, I went against the grain, popping a hood nigga's baby out. I was living the role of a typical baby momma.

My child's father made me hate his trifling, controlling ass. Yeah, I will admit I was angry, bitter, and resentful, but Renard tried his best to break me down first. This dude did some foul shit. Let me go down the degrading list: I was manipulated, humiliated, dissed and talked about, abandoned, and worst of all combined, stripped of my self-esteem and self-worth. Now, with that being said, please believe every bitch has their breaking point, and not all cards can be played. I'd gone from the convenient, common baby momma to the most ruthless. I went straight new jack on Renard and the pawns in my path. Fuck taking sympathy; I was out to ruin his life, 'cause never once did he really give a fuck about mine.

You can call a bitch crazy. You can say it was temporary insanity and that I lost my mind. Whatever the case, I snapped and set the shit off. Yeah, I'm sure you'll pass your judgments, but I don't give a fuck. I was tired of being taken advantage of and treated like a little piece of shit by him and his popcorn groupies. For me to be the mother of his child, I should've carried some weight and gotten more loyalty. As far as I'm concerned, they all had it coming, and I ain't never saying sorry. The bastard can rot in hell for all I care!

Yeah, yeah, yeah, I know that for every action comes a reaction, but I'll deal with my bridge when it's time to cross. Till then, I'll be pleading not guilty to this judge on every single charge. I cannot wait to get up out this filthy orange County jumpsuit, because please believe I'd do every single thing I did out of rage all over again. Love fucked me, and I ran it the hell over.

Now, close yo' mouth, pump yo' brakes, and slow yo' roll before you end up in the same position I just put Nardo in. Don't judge me, because nine out of ten times, you would have done the same fuckin' thing if it happened to you. So, pay attention and listen up. This is how it began.

CHAPTER ONE

Zaria

As soon as Nardo texted back that he was on his way, it felt like there were butterflies swarming around in my stomach. As angry as I was at him, I couldn't help but to love and lust for him. I leaped up from the couch and started getting my house in order. Me and my li'l momma had been cooped up in the living room, having multiple Netflix-and-chill binges for the last few days, and it was obvious. There were dirty bottles, soiled diapers, onesies that Cidney had spit up on, empty snack wrappers scattered everywhere, and dirty dishes stacked on the table. Nardo would read me for filth if he saw how trifling I was living, instead of blaming himself for helping me sink so low. The more freedom he took, the less secure about our future I felt. He and I might not have had the best relationship before I got pregnant, but he at least came around. Since our daughter's birth, though, he hadn't played the role as a family man but a couple of times, and that had been just to drop off some formula, diapers, and a few dollars. Not only was I feenin' for some fresh air and a break from motherly duties, but for some attention that only a man could give a woman. Renard and his stroke were all I knew. We'd been off-and-on for more than eight years.

Me and Nardo hooked up as teenagers, and it was unconventional. I met him through my ex-best friend

Melanie while they were still dating, then took him from her effortlessly. Call it being fake or phony; it is what it is. I took her man because she couldn't keep her mouth closed from being braggadocious. She told me how long Nardo's pipe was and how he stroked her pussy, how much money he spent on her weekly for her hair and nails, and how they would go shopping on Sundays to run through the dope money he made all week on the corner. Her stories not only kept my attention, but they fascinated me to the point of wanting to know what it would be like to walk in her shoes through the mall on a Sunday morning. So, I cut into Nardo, and I haven't looked back since.

The entire process was like taking candy from a baby, since I knew how freaky he liked to get, even down to the details of what Melanie wouldn't do. I made sure he was sexually pleased every day and several times throughout it. Women are thirsty creatures, always checking for the next chick's man, her goods, and comparing it to what they have on deck. I was no different, and the term "best friend" was just a label. It was better that I taught Melanie that lesson at an early age before she got her heart broken as a bitter old bitch. I'd publicly embarrassed and betrayed Melanie for love, money, and sex—and I'd do it again. I don't care how much turmoil me and Nardo have been through over the last eight years.

Like every new relationship, he and I experienced the honeymoon period where everything was solid and all good. I was young, dumb, and living on a cloud like our love was more important than life itself. We went out to eat and to the movies all the time. I got gifts even when I didn't ask for them, and he never talked out of line to me in front his boys. I was his wifey, and everybody in the hood respected it, which was bonus because my parents kept their ear to the streets.

My mom quickly approved of Nardo once my hand flew out of her purse and into his pocket. She even taught me the rules of the game to pass down to him, so he'd level up from the small-time hustler he was. Shit was sweet until he and his boy hit a lick. Renard went from getting little-boy money to grown-man money, and then came the hoes. The more options he got, the more he took, and the more I fought. I was determined not to lose the man I'd made.

Once the house was in order and smelling fresh, I jumped in the shower and started my glow-up process. I'd been lounging in my favorite pair of sweat pants and an oversized, holey T-shirt all day, plus I'd worked up a funky sweat from cleaning up. The massaging flow of hot water felt good crashing against my skin. The steam was low key putting me to sleep. Had Nardo not been on his way, I would've run a piping hot Jacuzzi bath to soak and relax my nerves. Cidney had cried all morning and had me about to drop her off at the police precinct. I'd be a deadbeat mom if it wasn't for Netflix having each season of PBS's *Sid the Science Kid* loaded. My baby can't even crawl and she's addicted to the shit. I don't know what that li'l dude and his gang did to her psyche, but she was settled and into a nap by the second episode.

After a few more minutes of standing under the shower head, I douched then thoroughly washed my cootie cat with a plain white bar of antibacterial Dial soap. I don't play when it comes to catching yeast infections, so I saved the melon daiquiri scented body wash for my skin and the lotion and body spray for the finishing touches. Nardo hadn't seen my naked body since it bounced back, and I wanted it to be one-hundred percent right. I was looking crazy the last time he stopped by to drop Cidney off some Tylenol to help break her shot-induced fever, and I hadn't even cared about putting Vaseline on my crusty lips. I was planning on using sex as my secret weapon and my pussy as the take-down ammunition tonight, though. My baby daddy had never been able to turn me down when a nut was involved, and I hoped tonight was no different. I was aching for his stroke.

The house was still quiet when I finished in the bathroom, so I tiptoed to my room and closed the door. I didn't want to wake Cidney while I listened to music and got cute for her daddy's visit. The first thing I did was take my head scarf so my hair wouldn't sweat out, then took the flexi rods out so my curls could start falling. I knew they'd be perfectly cascading down my back by the time Nardo arrived, which was exactly what I wanted. I was initially upset about having to pay over two hundred dollars for a bundle of weave, but I was happy that I'd sprung for the grade-A human hair. To say it was worth every dime is an understatement. I'd gotten it sewn in a month before my due date, and it was still silky without me having to add any sheen. All I had to do was slick down a few loose edges with some olive oil edge control, and then the entire style was on point.

Instead of getting fully dressed, I kept it simple with a cute, two-piece lavender pajama set that I hadn't worn since before I got pregnant. Except for my breasts that were fuller and filling out the top, and my juicy booty cheeks that were spilling out of the shorts, the leftover ten pounds of pregnancy weight I was still carrying had the cotton material clinging to my skin like a glove. I'd always had a thick frame, but I was now thicker than a Snicker and loving it. I couldn't wait to see Nardo's reaction.

Damn, where is this nigga at anyway? I looked at the text message's time and added up how long it had been. I was tempted to send a message asking for his whereabouts or at least his estimated time of arrival, but

I didn't want to jinx a good thing before it got to happen. I'd been trying my hardest to get Renard and me back to the honeymoon stage of our relationship. I grew up with my father, and it would be nice if my daughter could grow up with hers. I was tired of hearing my momma talk shit about me not being able to keep my family together like she kept hers. *Oh, well, trust the process.* I tried not getting in my feelings over my mom's opinion, or anyone else's for that matter. Me and Nardo might not have the best dynamic, but it was ours.

Once I was fully put together, I stood in the full-length mirror and took a bunch of selfies and a gang more pictures that showed how stacked my body was looking. I then posted them to my favorite social media site so any lurker that I had could see I wasn't over here looking like a dried-up old maid. After the Melanie situation, I didn't bond with many females, but I had made more than my share of enemies. It had been eight years, and girls from around the way still wanted me to fall off. After I posted the pictures, I then made a status that it was about to be family time around my crib and to look forward to a family photo within a few hours. I didn't care how petty it may have seemed; I was letting the world know that I still fucked with Nardo heavy. With me and him being so off-and-on and him being all of a sudden so distant, I knew chicks were gunning for my position even more. Hoes lived by the "out of sight, out of mind" logic more than niggas did. My man wasn't for everybody, though.

Cidney started fussing as soon as I got done, which was perfect timing, but terribly wrong at the same time.

"Oh, no, baby girl. It is not time to get up yet." I dashed to her nursery then quietly tiptoed to her crib.

Her nursery was peaceful, serene, and my favorite room in the house. I'd fallen asleep more than a few times in her rocking chair. It was painted light pink but decorated in several shades of purple, and had teddy bears, stars, and princess tiaras all over the walls. I even had my nail tech design each letter in Cidney's name for the wall as well. I'd taken a theme I'd seen on the internet, put my own spin to the vision, and then ran through over a thousand dollars of Nardo's money making sure I didn't miss a detail. He didn't let our beef get in the way of him doing for his seed, and I took full advantage of his heart. I even had an over-the-top baby shower and invited a bunch of bitches I didn't have a bond with so I could floss. No matter what went on and was said behind my back, actions spoke louder than words, and I wanted the truth on the floor. Cidney was my link to Nardo for the rest of his life. My baby shower was our marriage in my mind.

I didn't want Cidney to wake all the way up if she wasn't ready to, since I was trying to get some one-on-one time with her father, so I flipped on the musical projector. I was hoping the lullabies could help sing her back into a slumber. I was well overdue for some coddling of my own. It had been just me and her roughing it out day in and out for the last week.

"Mommy needs you to go back to sleep for just a little while longer." I sounded foolish trying to compromise with a baby, but I was desperate. She was sucking her tiny lips and trying to put her itty-bitty fingers into her mouth. I knew she wasn't hungry because she hadn't started crying yet, so I searched around the bedding for her pacifier and let it soothe her back to sleep. I knew better than to spoil her, which was why I also made sure Nardo bought me every knick-knack, gadget, bouncer, and nurturing item they had on the market for newborns. I wasn't trying to have a brat that my mom wouldn't babysit. She didn't let one day of my pregnancy pass by that she didn't remind me of her being too young to be somebody's grandma.

Nardo, on the other hand, was good to me during the pregnancy. Not only did he make sure I kept a refrigerator of food, fruit, and junk that I had cravings for, but he also made sure to pick up all my carryout orders. I got super big carrying her because I was hungry all the time. The only reason Nardo knew I was not lying and didn't give me a hard time when I called him for a food run was that he saw me eat it all. Hell, he'd be here, and we'd be cuddled up on the couch, and I'd order in delivery or beg him to cook.

On the day of my baby shower, he'd showed up and out for the whole hood and my family. At first, I was stomping around that day with my lips in a frown because he kept answering the phone saying he was on the way but not showing up. It was heavy on my mind that he was cuddled up with his ex-girlfriend, keeping her cool since she had threatened to run up on me at my baby shower. Though I wasn't the least bit worried about Mel as far as throwing hands with her goes, I was worried that Nardo wanted some pussy that was not waddling around. Okay, maybe he wasn't all the way good while I was pregnant.

Closing Cidney's door quietly, I was about to call Nardo to find out where he was at when my windows started rattling. I peeked out just in time to see Nardo swerve up to the curb in his triple-black Range Rover on chrome wheels with his radio turned up to the max. Always bold and making a statement, he backed up into my driveway and kept the music blasting, disturbing my working-class neighbors.

Knowing the routine, I watched him pick up his phone and probably check in with the newest hoe. I was really trying hard not to let that bitch ruin my time with him. Since our breakup, she'd become a constant thorn, always hating when he came over or did financially for me and Cid. I couldn't wait to go for that hoe. Yeah, he was giving her the wife life now, but me and him shared a seed, something more than she could claim title to. Little did she know I was out to reclaim my throne.

As I discreetly peeked out the window, watching the man I loved, I couldn't help but to think back on what had originally brought us together. Melanie used to kick it with him back in the day when we were teenagers and he wasn't nothing but a low-level drug dealer that worked for another worker who was allowed to have a worker. Renard started so low on the totem pole that the police never ran up on him when they raided all the other bag boys. He wasn't even worthy of them trying to flip into a snitch. Nardo wasn't getting money; only hand-me-downs from other hustlers and maybe a fresh pair of tennis shoes if they were feeling friendly. I knew how empty his pockets were because my ex-best friend used to kick it with him. Lucky for me, that all changed, and by the time he was getting real money, he was mine.

As he boldly stepped into the threshold of the house he'd cashed out on for me and Cid, I smiled sweetly, hoping to start our quality time on a good note. His Polo Blue cologne smelled so fucking good. I loved a man who kept his smell-good game great! Nardo had on a black pair of True Religion cargo shorts, a new out-of-the package wife beater, and some crispy retro Jordans. With his beard thick and trimmed neatly, perfection was a must with him, and I was sure he'd just hopped out of his barber's chair.

"Hey, daddy, I missed you," I whispered into his ear, throwing my arms around his waist. Hugging him tightly, I didn't want to let go. "We both missed you."

Nardo being Nardo, he barely responded to my desperate moves of affection. He was intent on being hardcore to the bitter end. He hugged me back with little emotion, making me feel slightly insignificant.

"Now you miss a nigga? Yo' ass is crazy for real, Zaria. Where was all that wife-like emotion earlier when you was going ham on a nigga voice mail?" His deep baritone voice sent chills up and down my spine, even though he was calling me out on acting so elementary.

"Well, that was then. You know I be tripping when you don't answer the phone. It could be an emergency with the baby, and you're laid up with some ratchet ho." Lowering my voice to a murmur at the end, I didn't want him to think I was trying to trip or start an argument.

"Look, don't start no shit with me, Z. I didn't respond to your little drama earlier for a reason. You can miss me with all that because my mood ain't no lighter for it now."

"Naw, Nardo, I'm cool, and we're cool. You can trust that I'm not trying to get on your bad side. You know how I can get over you, babe. It's just love." My mind started to race and ponder on what ways I could get back into his good graces, having reminded him of my nagging ways.

It was his fault I was cut like that anyway. Had it not been so easy for me to steal him from Mel, I would've had faith in our relationship standing strong through rough patches. However, Nardo continuously reminded me of his boss status in the streets. It was not a hood heffa walking who didn't want a part of him. The more he crept, the more I clowned. Even though my moms thought I was as dumb as a bag of rocks for him, there was no way I was gonna diss my baby daddy.

Nardo quickly pushed past me to get into the living room. I had mango butter oil burning throughout the house, mainly because that was his favorite scent. I liked to keep him comfortable in hopes of making his visits last longer. Anything I could try to get my family back together was worth it in my book.

"Where's my little mama?" he asked, glancing around the room, taking off his shoes and making himself comfortable. "I miss my little princess."

"I put her down for a nap about a good forty-five minutes ago. She's been kinda cranky today, so let's just leave her be," I schemed, sitting down across from him with my legs folded Indian style.

"No complaints here. You know a nigga hate all that whining and shit. But I guess she gets that crap from her mother, though," he fired back, still continuing to be an asshole.

This fool ain't been here but three minutes and already his smart comments have weighed in on me. I was not in the mood for his antics or his criticism. He was the main reason I was always nagging and bitching anyway. Nardo had a bad tendency to creep out on me, and he thought I was dumb as a bag of rocks. So, fuck yeah, my attitude stayed on trip mode. Guess you lose 'em the same way you get 'em.

Now, Renard's reputation in the street couldn't be challenged, from his physique to his hood hustle. He was six feet even and muscular, with a peanut butter complexion damn near covered in tattoos. You would've thought he had an addiction to the shit. With dark brown, dreamy eyes and waves so laid they'd make you seasick, my child's father carried himself like a true boss, making bitches and hoes alike want to be on his arm. I watched 'em come and go, but because I'd hatched the golden egg—our baby girl Cidney—Nardo was stuck with me for life. I didn't care how he thought the game would be played.

"So, what's been good on the block?" I asked, wanting him to entertain me with the antics of the hood. I'd truly been bored.

"You know how it is, and ain't shit changed but the day," he grunted. "The same cats who were struggling are still struggling, and the same muthafuckas who were up are still looking down. Me and Izzi are about to shake some thangs up, though." He held back on the details.

"Whatchu mean by shake thangs up?" I was interested. "Y'all got a beef going?"

"You know me, making this bread, my baby. It's come-up season on these streets."

"I feel you on that. I'm looking for a come-up too." I giggled sexily, hoping he was catching on. I needed Nardo's money to get outfits for me and Cidney, and from past experience, I knew the best way to his pockets was through his pants zipper.

"Oh, is that so?" He leaned back onto my nutmeg-colored leather couch, adjusting the way his sac was positioned. "Ain't shit good when your slick ass is on the prowl."

Snickering, I hoped that was a sign of his mood improving for the better.

"I don't know what that is supposed to mean, but me and Cid need some new clothes for this photo shoot I booked earlier," I whined, giving him the sad face. Back in the day, playing the helpless little girl role got me more Guess jean jacket outfit sets than Hudson's department store kept in stock.

"Damn, Z." He got excited. "So, I'm your come-up, huh? You stay deep in a nigga pockets fa sho'. What happened to the stack of cash I left your hot ass the last time I was over here? I ain't your muthafucking Bank of America." he gritted his teeth, refusing to cut me any slack. "It ain't a time I've been over here that you haven't had your hand out."

"It only seems like that because you don't come over here but every thirty days." I exaggerated to make a point, then flipped the conversation. "Are you serious, Nardo? Because if so, you've got a lot of nerve. How am I supposed to get out and do anything when you don't even call to see Cidney, let alone come over here to watch her for me?"

I kept going. "Damn. You know I've got bills around this place." I played it off, knowing I'd jump fresh getting the new Soho metallic gray leather Gucci bag. Still, with the water and sewerage company's threatening shut-off notice only a few feet away, I was hoping he'd at least give me enough to make a payment arrangement. Otherwise, I'd be playing roommate at my mom's. It was nothing for me to blow his money on me looking like a million bucks, knowing he'd come through with the cash to replace it—even if I did have to suffer through him talking bullshit.

"I'm not playing with you, shorty. Matter of fact, download some work search apps onto your phone so you can do something more productive on it than calling me relentlessly. I set you up sweet with this house. The least you could do is get a hustle to pay the bills."

"Boy, stop it." I twirled one of my curls around my finger and giggled. "They'll foreclose on this house before I punch somebody's clock. I don't know shit about a shift." I wasn't raised by taxpaying parents.

"I bet you'd learn real fast once the bailiffs came to sit your bougie ass on the curb," he said.

"I'm not about to be punching no nine-to-five or midnight clock while you run around tossing money on butt-naked broads. When I do badly, Cid does bad." I felt the need to throw around my weight. He was tripping, and on that note, I couldn't bite my tongue. There was no way in hell my share of his cash would be divvied up through the hood.

"Girl, you're a mess fa sho'. What is your plotting ass gonna do when I give my princess a little brother or sister?" He grinned, knowing that slick-mouth shit would get under my skin.

I couldn't believe he had the audacity to come at me like that. "You ain't dumb enough to try it." I sucked my teeth, having caught a huge attitude, and I was ready to pop off. I'd never thought about him having a second child, but for sure if he did, my position would be downgraded even more.

"Man, quit it with that jaw-jacking and toss me that remote. You're a bad fucking experience that I ain't trying to have with two broads at the same time."

Grim-faced, I took his disrespect as another slap in the face. Renard was always slamming my ego into the gutter, but real talk, it was getting hard to rationalize with myself as to why I loved his ass so much. He could've gotten up and beaten the door down without a *"please, don't go"* from me. I threw the remote to him with all my might. He caught it before it hit him square in the chest.

"I was not a bad experience when we were making our daughter. I was not a bad experience when you were over here rubbing my belly, my feet, and polishing my toenails because I was too big to bend down and too tired to go to Kimmie. I don't care what you wanna say now to hurt my feelings. You definitely were not calling me a bad experience then."

"I was making sure my baby girl got here safely, Zaria. You be reading more words on the page when I present you with shit, and that's where the fuck-up be at." He kept crushing me with his truth.

"So, you don't love me? What we're going through is more than a break for us, to get right, to get back tighter?" I was choking on my words, getting ready to have a full-blown crying fit and tantrum if he said anything similar to "our breakup is permanent."

"Yeah, I love yo' ass, girl. Don't put no words in my mouth; just hear what I said. I ain't come over here to make you cry or argue, so please quit getting all sensitive. I see you're over there getting all fidgety." He shook his head, flicking the tuner over to Netflix.

"Like I ain't got a reason." I tried to stare at the flat screen and avoid looking at him head-on. "You're here, there, and everywhere but right here at home . . . like I ain't shit."

Angry and frustrated, my body shook from built-up tension. My plan hadn't been for me and my baby daddy to bump heads, but we were two combative personalities, and his insults were unnecessary.

"Aw, don't get to acting all sour and shit 'cause your sensitive ass can't take a joke."

"Well, I don't play like that." I folded my arms, continuing my tantrum.

"Yeah, whatever. I ain't trying to hear that old spoiled-girl routine. Get over here and give your manz some attention for these few dollars," he demanded, unfastening his huge brown Hermes belt buckle.

Even though I was infuriated, bottom line, I wanted that green paper and loved pleasing his black ass till he came. So, no doubt I gave in to his request and dropped down onto my knees.

"Yeah, girl, you know just how to work a nigga right. That good-good deep throat," he hummed as I slung his rod out of his Hanes boxers and tickled the tip of the swollen head.

The sooner I hit him off with a little of my head game, the sooner he'd fill my pockets up and I could be out the door and in the streets. Although I had been feenin' for his attention earlier, him saying he was not moving all the way back in had me only thinking of myself. My gynecologist did recommend I get a breather from Cidney to not experience postpartum depression or caretaker burnout. Besides all that, Nardo had become king of pulling double and triple overnight shifts away from dirty diapers, middle-of-the-night feedings, and Cid crying for no known reasons. He needed to get some daddy hours in and give me a break. Right after I sucked him to sleep, he'd be punching in for babysitting duty.

CHAPTER TWO

Nardo

"Yo, Zaria! grab li'l momma before she break a nigga's nap," I complained, then rolled over and smothered my face with a throw pillow. I hadn't planned on falling asleep on Zaria's couch, but I had, and I was trying to stay that way for a little while longer. The last thing I wanted to hear was a baby's relentless crying. "Hey, girl! I know you hear her crying. Quit being funny and get her before I get up and leave," I threatened. I knew Zaria wanted me around, just like I knew she liked to play games with a nigga.

I was irritated and wished I had stayed at the trap making money, or even at the crib with my new chick, Spice. It was now obvious Zaria had busted camp and left me alone with Cidney. I didn't hear any movement or sounds in the house, except the baby's cries, of course.

Damn, I've gotta learn how to keep my pants up and zipped around her nut-chasing ass. I felt played. I already knew Zaria had snuck out of there as soon as she swallowed my cum.

I lay on the couch, hoping Cidney would cry herself back to sleep, but I ended up running like lightning speed to her room once she started hyperventilating with her cry. I might not have known how to soothe her, but I fa damn sho' didn't want something happening to her on my clock. The last thing my dope-hustling ass needed was a child abuse charge. I was ready to knock Zaria's head off for being slick and leaving her baby alone with me. I might have played the role of Cidney's daddy, but I wasn't fa sho' if she was my seed. I was just being a stand-up dude since I knew that I'd stood up in her without a condom on plenty of times.

Cidney was tangled up in her receiving blanket and beet red by the time I made it to her crib. "Please, God, let her be straight," I prayed as I scooped her out of it and sat down in the rocking chair. I remembered putting this entire nursery together, from the paint down to the tiniest decoration. Zaria worked a nigga's back broke while she was knocked up, and had me crossing off days on my own calendar.

Although I wasn't sure if I was her father or not, I cradled Cidney close to my chest until she calmed down. I couldn't front and act like I didn't have an attachment to her or love her. I was by her momma's side when she was born.

"Hey, Princess. Daddy missed you." I finally took her off my chest and kissed her forehead. She smelled just like baby products. Crazy or not, Zaria had been taking great care of Cidney. That's the one thing I hadn't been able to complain about.

After Cidney made a few gurgling noises at me, she started back crying, but her screams got louder than they were when I first got woken up. I knew it was because she wasn't used to me and wanted her momma.

"It's okay, Princess. I want your stank-ass momma to get back here too." I empathized with her, then went in search for my cell phone.

I snatched it off the coffee table, entered the lock code, then hit SEND on Zaria's number on my home screen. "If she doesn't answer, though, I'm gonna take you to meet your soon-to-be step-mommy," I said out loud, knowing my secret was safe with Cidney.

After three or four rings, Zaria picked up, but I could barely hear her through Cidney's screams.

This babysitting shit is for the birds indeed, I thought to myself.

"Hello? Hello?" I tried screaming into the phone over Cidney.

"Hey, baby. What's up?" she nonchalantly questioned, not knowing how truly pissed I was at her.

"Don't 'yeah, what's up' me, girl. Where are you at?"

"Whoa!" she yelled into the phone. "Is that how you greet your child's mother? The one who pushed life out of her body after going through a rough pregnancy for your black, ungrateful ass?" She continued to drag that same tired story of her claim to fame into the ground.

"No, that is how I greet an ungrateful-ass woman who cannot stop playing immature games," I fired back. "I'm not trying to hear shit you are saying unless it is 'I am on my way,' Zaria. You hear this baby crying." I continued trying to rock and soothe our child to the best of my hood-hand ability. "So, get here and do yo' damn job. You were the one slipping on yo' pills for her, so you claim." I purposely pushed her buttons, still salty about the alleged birth control failure bullshit she'd served me along with the positive pregnancy test.

"Aw, nigga, shut up and miss me with all that bullshit you love to bring up from the past. If you didn't want a baby by me, you should have put a condom on. I never begged you to run up in me raw, nor did I hold you down while you filled me up with your sperm. You knew what you were doing."

"And you knew what you were doing when you told a nigga you were popping birth control pills but wasn't. I might be a street nigga, but I ain't dumb. I know you wasn't doing nothing but lying so I wouldn't strap up. So, with that being said, hurry up and bring your tricky ass back home to *your* daughter."

With Cidney refusing to stop fussing, I was unable to clearly think through one thought.

"Whatever. I will be there when I get there. Mommies need a break too," she annoyingly sang into the phone. It was obvious that Zaria was enjoying finally being able to force me into a corner. I was usually the one with the upper hand in our lopsided relationship.

"And what the fuck am I supposed to do with her and all this yelling?"

"Come on, Nardo. You are making this way harder than it should really be. Calming a cranky baby down is not a difficult task or as hard as you are making it. You do not need a rocket scientist's brain to figure the shit out." Zaria continued being disrespectful. "She is either wet or hungry. The diapers are in her bedroom, and the formula is in the kitchen." Zaria giggled her last few words before ending the call on me.

There was no need to wonder why I hadn't been around here hitting Zaria off. What guy doesn't want to lock and key their baby momma, cutting her off from the whole world? In my case, however, it was best just to pay and be gone. Besides, this responsibility shit was too far in for me. Calling her back, I was ready to go through the phone and snap her neck in two.

"Hey, man, look." I started off calmly, trying not to scare Cidney again. "You are really testing my patience. You already know how I hustle and that I have things to do. You are holding me up. Where in the fuck are you at so I can drop this baby off to you?" I asked through clenched teeth. I was ready to explode.

She burst out laughing. "I wish you would be that petty, Nardo. I'll see you later because right now, I'm at where I'm at and doing what I do."

"Quit playing games with me, Z. I swear fo' God, you pissing me off."

"Ugh, well you better get yo' attitude together real quick. I don't want that toxic vibe around my daughter." She giggled then hung up.

Oh, it was on. I couldn't wait to get my hands on her and teach her a well-deserved lesson. Playing me for a sucka was not an option I was willing to roll with.

Quit thinking with yo' dick. There was no one to blame but me. This was not her first act of bossiness, but I kept coming back for more. Arguing with her had become pointless. With her ghetto-girl attitude and the poisonous pussy between her legs, our relationship had become a constant battle of bickering and fucking.

She thought this bullshit was a joke. I had loot floating around in the streets to pick up, plus a life of my own. Babysitting was not involved in any part of my routine, so off rip I was on fire. She had some audacity and nerve to be out in the streets, blowing my cash and preventing me from making it at the same time.

I was growing weary of Zaria. With all the drama her spoiled ass was putting me through being insecure, a straight nagging bitch, but more than all my old-school chick, her days of pimping me for dollars and dick were numbered. If I would've known her cat trap was this polluted with problems, there was no way in hell she would've outshined Melanie.

Z once had strength and confidence, something I admired in my main girl, as I was a street hustler. My life in the hood depended on a girl that could keep it rough, real, and cutthroat. She once held me down and showed me the utmost respect. Up until she waddled up to me knocked up, I thought I'd chosen a winner. Zaria was cute, nothing super spectacular to write home about, but she was loyal to the team, no questions asked. With me, that went far in the game.

But as of late, I was tired of constantly defending myself to her and dealing with the calculated tantrums. Hell yeah, I was stepping out and slinging my dick with other chicks. I am a man, and keeping it one-hundred, we need different pussy flavors on a regular to keep shit in our worlds settled. Zaria should have been playing the role I had designed for her as my wifey, instead of trying to be my master and leash a dog down.

Looking down at a semi-settled Cidney, I stared at her closely, searching for one feature, one baby hair, or one small facial expression that mirrored mines. I'd never had a paternity test and was just going off of Zaria's word, praying that this child was not a scheme or plot for continued cash flow. Seeing nothing but her mom's traits, I pitied the little girl, knowing she would grow up just like the skeezer who'd gotten lucky enough to steal and trap me.

Feeling my phone vibrating, I hurried to snatch it from my holster, fearing it would throw her into another tantrum.

"Yo, what it do, boss?" Izzi said.

"Shit, I can't call it. Zaria done up and pulled a shake move on me while I was passed out. Ain't no telling when she plans on marching back in here, so I'm stuck with the baby till whenever." I accepted the bittersweet reality. I couldn't stand letting my money dangle in the streets, but if this was my daughter, not being a part of her life was not an option.

"Well, it ain't nothing but business on this end, dude. You already know I'm holding the block down and keeping these boys in line." He referenced the small crew we ran.

Izzi was a goon, my partner in the crime-infested streets of Detroit, and my right-hand man. It was not nothing I didn't trust him with, and I knew he had the block sewn up and on lock.

"A'ight, cool. I ain't worried. I'm more than pissed that her ass caught me slipping." My aggravation was clear, but my manz already knew what popped between me and Zaria.

"I feel you. Baby momma is always putting you through the wringer. I see your strong arm is weak."

"Later for all that. This about to be her last show with my ass. I'm 'bout fed up with her fuckin' games."

"All right, guy. Enough of that loddy-doddy babble, man, because you ain't through. So, when you break free from diaper camp, I'll be on the block. And try not to get caught slipping next time," Izzi jokingly warned before hanging up the phone.

After laying Cidney down into one of the many cradle, comfort, shut-a-baby-up gadgets her moms had forced me to buy so she could front at the baby shower, I turned the volume on the television down then got back comfortable on the couch. I might've tripped about spending a grip on her furniture back when she was whining for a luxury set, but the money was well worth it. I maxed and relaxed like a king whenever I came to smash.

Checking my missed calls and texts, I knew I was not the only one pissed by Zaria temporarily sitting me down. Spice, my island jump-off chick, had been calling my cell repeatedly for the last hour and texting to ask what time I would be home. I had met her during Zaria's last trimester of pregnancy and had been fucking around with her since the baby actually dropped. Her son had been begging to meet Cidney since he saw a picture of her.

Spice knew about Zaria and that I visited with Cidney for a few hours through the week, but she was not down with the sister-wives sensation. Though she had been understanding, taking major losses on account of trying to stand by my side while I stood strong by Zaria's for Cidney, Spice would be screaming my ear off and begging to tag along whenever I came over here if she knew I was still slipping up in Zaria. I was having my cake and eating at the same time, with two loyal women.

Spice and Zaria were similar in a lot of ways. They both had feisty personalities, short tempers, and were possessive over their man. They both went against their families to be with me. Whereas Zaria's relationship with her mother had healed over time, Spice's father still had not forgiven her, and she was still suffering behind his decision.

Spice's father was gang affiliated and a true narcotics trafficker. I had no idea Spice was raised by or even knew a Jamaican don when I approached her big-booty ass. I found out when he came through her door and slapped her around for sleeping with a black man that was born on American soil. Spice's father did not care that I pushed dope to put food into my mouth and clothes onto my back, but he fa sho' cared that his youngest daughter was going against the grain by not being with a man from their culture.

Her family was not enthused by her choice to raise their only grandson out of true Jamaican culture and on American soil, but deserting the man who'd stolen her heart and pumped her pussy dry was a joke she refused to take seriously. She was cut off for a punishment, which sank Spice. Growing up, he'd made it possible for Spice to be wealthy, have tokens and small treasures from all over the world, and to be educated alongside the country's most political elite citizens. If she wanted to squander that with the less fortunate and those beneath her bloodline against his wishes, he couldn't tolerate the continued connection. I'd been holding her down heavy ever since. We'd been clear, with no beefs, since I looked out for her little boy, but lately she'd been on a nigga tough about making us one hundred percent official.

"Oh, boy. Look who decided to come back to life." As any female I dealt with hated me disappearing, she was no different.

"Yeah, what's happening, ma?"

"Nothing, but I have been blowing your phone up for almost two hours," she slightly overexaggerated. "Where are you?" I could hear the honest-given feistiness she'd inherited from her pops ready to come out.

"I'm locked down with the baby right now, and after that, I've gotta catch up with Izzi on the block." I shut down her hopes of me coming straight to her neck of the woods for a quickie.

Even though Zaria made my nerves boil, she'd set me straight and proper with her head game. I was not in a rush to get home and get a nut off with Spice. That was the greatest perk of having two main women.

"I wish you would kick her ass to the curb already," Spice argued. "She is always pulling some ol' off-the-wall type shit. These American girls can be so uncouth." To hear her go in on Zaria could be hilarious at times.

I held Spice and her kid down. Li'l fella even looked at me like a daddy. I would be damned if my own blood child couldn't call me out like he could. I was quick to put her in her place.

"Naw, never that. You already know me and my baby moms are gonna keep it tight for the little one. The bitch makes me sick, but I will not leave her out here on the solo tip struggling." I kept it real, cutting eyes over at Cidney. "I'm not even cut like that. And since I kick it with your son, you should be happy that I'm not."

"Me being thankful and stupid are two different things, Renard. Of course I am thankful for you being there for my son, but please don't mistake the two." She was starting to sound like Zaria. "Be honest with me if you are banging her, because it seems like you are." Spice caught me off guard. "I don't care what you say, because I am close to giving you an ultimatum that involves you having to make a choice to stay away from there. You can petition the court for parental rights and cut her ass out." Spice sounded like she was outlining a weekly task list for me.

"Hey, we can kill this conversation now that you brought up court. Even Zaria knows to keep the law and its affiliates up out of my business." Taking a few deep breaths, I was trying to gain some control so I didn't blow up on Spice. "Listen up. You do not know me as well as you think you know me if you think trying to control the moves I make with ol' girl is an option. You don't have that power and never will. I'm not about to run my GPS coordinates down to you or anyone else." I instantly got pissed because she was starting to remind me of Zaria's crazed ass.

As the line went silent, my island honey was hanging onto every word falling from my lips. One ego-having, wannabe-alpha woman was allowed to speak out of turn, and I was fighting tooth and nail to get her under control. Spice didn't have room for slip-ups, please believe.

"Like I said earlier, I'll be through there later tonight." Spice needed a reminder that I was not for the games and bullshit she was accustomed to dishing out to the peasants in her hometown. Dexter ran through my veins, and that made me more vengeful than any dread-rocking wannabe on any day.

"Have it your way. I'm about to walk into the nail salon and get pampered since you're not home to make me feel good." She still continued to get salty, not expecting me to have a face-to-face conversation with her later.

Today was not gonna be labeled as the day both chicks I banged played me for some punk-type-ass nigga. Naw, this wasn't it!

"I suggest you take some down time and get that little island attitude under check. I mean it." Ending the call and tossing the phone back onto the coffee table, I saw Cid scramble and suggest she might soon be waking up. I couldn't wait to bust camp and get back to handling business in the streets. Everything was off.

Leaning back and folding my arms, I began to watch the clock, becoming enraged with each tick. It was well after three o'clock, and Zaria hadn't called back or walked through the door. Something deep in my bones told me that when she did, it was gonna be some heavyweight furniture moving going down.

CHAPTER THREE

Zaria

Tossing my phone into the brand-new bag I purchased with a few of the dollars I'd slipped from Nardo's pocket, I rolled my eyes and took a few deep breaths. I had to calm myself down and control the urge I was feeling to call him back and go straight the hell off. I had been enjoying the small window of time I'd had out of the house not having to carry around a car seat. I did not realize how much I missed rolling the windows down and letting my hair fly with the wind to some loud-ass R&B or rap blaring through the speakers.

Right after I finished pleasing Nardo with some lip, mouth, tongue, and throat action, I had slipped some cash out of his pocket and then went out the front door just as I'd planned all along. The few hundred bucks treated me to a cute little purse, a matching pair of sandals, and some new outfits to stunt in. Although I have a head full of long hair, I love experiencing different styles and changing up my look. I will rock a bun with a bang, a sew-in down to my ass, and even a twenty-seven-piece short-do if the cosmetologist can lay the tracks properly. The only thing I will not do is walk around looking like a box of Crayola exploded on top of my head.

Hitting rewind and playback on my car radio, I turned the volume up to the max and started back singing along with my jam. K. Michelle knows she can hit some helluva notes and have a sister feeling empowered and all black girl magically, which is exactly what I needed to feel right about now. When Nardo wasn't working my body out, he was working my nerves out and giving me migraines. I might be wrong as hell for how I dipped out, leaving him with Cidney, but it was not like I had a kid on him and needed a babysitter. She was just as much his responsibility as she was mine. It was a shame that Nardo couldn't be a grown man on his own.

Scrolling through all the likes and comments underneath the selfies I'd posted to Facebook earlier, I then uploaded one of the pictures I'd snuck and snapped of Nardo laid out on my couch, snoring. The cryptic caption I typed was for my lurkers and his hoes. It read: **Daddy duty wears him out.** If any of them were smarter than a bag of rocks, they would put two and two together and notice Cidney was nowhere in the picture.

I would've walked out the acetone-smelling nail shop had my homegirl not owned it. There were young girls in every chair and even a couple that were lapped up. It seemed like everyone from the hood was trying to get their nail designs slayed by Kimmie, and I couldn't blame them. Hands down, she was the baddest nail tech in the metro-Detroit area. She had her own style, flair, and lane in the game. She even had the young black girls that were killing the nail game on their toes, and she stole their loyal customers from time to time. Though an overflowing shop was good for Kimmie's business, it wasn't good for my time. I wouldn't wait on a normal day, and definitely not with Nardo at home pitching a fit about having to keep his own child.

"Hey, Sue." I greeted Kimmie's cousin. Sue didn't do nails. She did lashes, eyebrows, and bikini waxes. I'd gotten her to do my lashes once or twice, but I wasn't about to take my panties off in this muthafucka. "Where's my homegirl at?" I asked her loudly, not because English wasn't her first language, but because I wanted everyone to know that me and Kimmie were cool.

"Her had to take phone call. She in back but be out in minute."

I was glad it wasn't hard to decipher what she'd said. Some of Kimmie's family couldn't put two syllables together without it still sounding like Korean gibberish.

"Oh, okay. Well, I'll wait right here." Instead of penning my name down on the sign-in sheet, I leaned onto the counter and boldly looked around the room like I owned the place. I then tipped my foot up so my red sole would show to all the eyes that were locked in on me. The simple move spoke volumes, and I never had a problem with being petty.

It didn't take long for Kimmie to come from the back. I had to stop myself from laughing because I'd never seen a foreigner like Kimmie—and I'm not trying to be funny. She swore she was an African American bombshell stuck in a Korean body. She had on a pair of too-tight denim jeans, a crop top, a pair of red bottom Louboutin sneakers, and her fly-away hair was French braided to the back in six corn rows. I'd never seen her dressed up like her ancestry, even with her people owning beauty supply stores and having the direct connection to all the bootleg shit that's shipped in from overseas, and I'd been rocking with Kimmie for years. She was always put together better than most of the chicks I grew up with.

"Hey, Kimmie-boo. Did you miss me?"

"Um, nope. Not as much as I missed me godbaby. Where Seed-knee at?" She was trying to say Cidney, but it sounded more like *seed* and *knee* put together.

"At home with her daddy." I said it like Nardo was happy about it. "And I sho' can't tell that you miss her. You ain't been over to see her since I came home from the hospital." I rolled my neck.

"You see dis shop. Me be so tired after I close that I would sleep here if me wouldn't get robbed." She always joked about a hood nigga running up on her, but she wouldn't be laughing if it were to happen for real.

"Blah, blah, blah. Save the excuses, Kimmie. Just put me in a chair and whip me up real quick so I can get back home. All I need is a pedicure and a manicure."

She twisted her face up at my request. "A manicure? Since when you don't get long nail? You know me can't put no boring manicure on flyer. Me need fly, flashy, funky nail."

"I know, I know. And I've got you once I get the hang of changing diapers. But for now, I've gotta keep it short and simple so I don't scratch her all up. I had to pop my whole set off in the hospital and was mad about it." I remembered my nailbeds aching.

"Ohhh, okay. Me understand. For Seed-knee, I get it. You gotta take care of baby right way. But have seat and I'll do you next. Give me fifteen minutes, 'kay?" She pointed her nail brush at me, seeing my irritation growing with each word that she said.

I hated not getting my way, especially since I wasn't trying to go sit in the lame section with the girls I'd just thrown shade at. I put my hand to my forehead and started rubbing my temples. I was being a real brat.

"If you're longer than fifteen minutes, I'm gonna make you do a house visit, plus make you bring along some egg rolls." I finally took a seat in one of the few aluminum folding chairs that were available.

"Behave, Z-gurl. You so crazy." She laughed. "Fifteen minutes." She then went to work on her client.

At the end of the day, I couldn't block Kimmie's money, especially since she was taking a risk in having a client walk out because I was clearly walking in and over someone who'd already been waiting. There was a Korean-owned and run nail shop on almost every corner in the hood, and for sure in every newly built plaza. When it came to getting money, Kimmie and her other Korean friends didn't care what risks they had to take. Although the west side of Detroit was known as the best side, it was still full of thugs and savages. Any one of these women could've raised up on Kimmie if they wanted to.

I listened to Kimmie rap to the Jay-Z song that was playing through the radio as she whipped some cold-ass nail art onto the perfectly laid acrylic. I couldn't wait to get in her seat. My nailbeds and cuticles were starving for her attention.

Kim Lee Won had been hooking my nails up since me and Nardo had been kicking it, and through all our many breakups. I kept her around for the gossip and for whatever information she could give me on him. More gossip came through her door than strip clubs and beauty salons combined. People never suspected a gang of Koreans would run back and repeat their stories when they came in gossiping, but Kimmie could translate everything her people couldn't run back in perfect English. Kimmie was my ratchet tale encyclopedia.

The overhead chimes rang, signaling that the door had opened, and distracted me from checking Kimmie. I looked up to see who was coming through it to a semi-familiar face, and my eyes ended up getting locked in on her. I hate when females stare, but I couldn't stop. There was something about her. She didn't have the same aura as the rest of us girls from the hood who were sitting in the waiting area, even with the tacky red- and cognac-colored braids that were in her head.

Hmm, well, damn. I wonder what nigga is her sponsor, I thought to myself as I sized her up. Even though she didn't know how to put her expensive pieces together, everything she was dressed in was name brand. She had on Prada shades, some Gucci sandals that I wouldn't have been caught dead in because of the large sole, and she was carrying a Chanel bag that was worth more than my mortgage and bill money for the month.

"Excuse me. How long of a wait is it for a full-service treatment?" The woman's thick Jamaican accent took me by surprise.

Rude as she could be, Kimmie slammed the clear coat of nail polish onto the nail table and scooted her chair over to the counter. "You see it's packed in here, honey, so it'll be at least an hour before you can start soaking your feet." Kimmie then slid back to her customer without waiting to see if the mystery lady would respond. I had to bite the insides of my cheeks to keep from laughing. Kimmie's ego could be a bit much to digest if you weren't cool with her. She never acted pressed for someone's business.

The mystery lady wasn't moved by Kimmie's obnoxiousness. She snickered, pushed her sunglasses to the top of her head, then started looking for an empty seat. I don't know if my pregnancy hormones were still in full swing, but my stomach started churning once she plopped down next to me. Her perfume reeked like she'd drenched herself in multiple brands just like her clothes.

"Hi, how are you doing?" There was a hint of mockery in her voice, like she'd picked up on my vibe.

"Huh? Excuse me? Are you talking to me?" I rose my eyebrows at her, completely caught off guard. Friendliness is not something you find in the hood.

"Um, yeah. I didn't mean no harm by it. I was just speaking since I'd sat right next to you," she casually responded then ran her fingers through her tacky braids.

"Oh, okay." I didn't greet her back but continued to give her the dumb look. For some reason, her vibes weren't sitting right with my instincts.

"A'ight, brat, you come now." Kimmie waved me to the pedicure chair and started filling up the bowl. "You lucky me love you, 'cause if me didn't, I wouldn't put you in front of no customer. Me love slaying you nails, but me hate taming yo' big ol' elephant feet." She put me on blast, making both her family and the other clients laugh.

"Ha-ha-ha, Kimmie. I see you're laughing, but I'm not. Don't make me accidentally kick you with my big elephant foot while I'm getting it tamed either. I'm not here for the jokes." I got up in the massage chair and dipped my feet into the warm water. "Unh-uh! You better make this water hotter, heifer. Please focus on doing your job and do it right." I purposely complained so she'd remember who was servicing who.

"Ohhh! You acting up today, Z-gurl." She was overly animated. "Come on and put you graceful foot up here so I can get to work." She slid her face mask up and started filing away.

I wonder if Cidney is driving her daddy up a wall. That's what his ass gets. If he came around more often, he would know how to deal with his daughter. Oh, well, I thought as she started removing my worn polish.

"So, hey, home girl, me been missing you ass down here. The baby have you super busy, huh?" She laughed.

"Yeah, something like that. Sometimes she be crying for no damn reason at all, but I guess that's what a newborn does." I got irritated thinking about all the broken sleeps and restless nights I'd had since giving birth, then even more annoyed when I thought about how many peaceful sleeps Renard had gotten since Cidney had made her arrival.

"Aww, Z, dang. That why me don't have no baby yet. Me need me beauty rest. So how Nardo with Seed-knee? He acting like daddy supposed to act?"

I tried not taking her question for shade.

I licked my lips and braced myself to tell a stream of lies. Cool or not, I wouldn't dare tell her the truth about how dismissive and disrespectful he'd been acting. "I can't complain. He's been taking care of business and holding me down. Cidney loves her daddy so much that she disses me when he comes over." It felt good to fluff the truth and exaggerate.

"Hmm, okay. If you say so." She blew my last words off then moved on to some juicer tea. "So, have you bump heads with Miss Mel lately?"

The mere mention of my boyfriend's ex-girlfriend irked me. "Nope, but I wouldn't mind if I did. She had a lot to say when I was pregnant and couldn't throw these hands, so I'd like to see if she's as cocky now that I'm back on my A-game," I said, referencing my body's bounce-back.

"You need not fight over man, because that be stupid. I say both of you mend friendship and kick Nardo dumb ass." Kimmie rolled her eyes and waved her file at me in a circular motion. "Him foul like old fish in river."

I wanted to laugh at her analogy, but she was out of line, and I couldn't tolerate the outright blatant disrespect. Good, bad, or indifferent, Nardo was still my daughter's father. "Yo, Kimmie, chill out. That's still my baby daddy." I chin-checked her ass quick, fast, and in a hurry. "You don't hear me commenting about Chin's tight pants and too-little flip flops." I might've been bold, but she needed to see how it felt for me to talk so rude and reckless. Giving her back the eye roll she'd just dished out, I was ready to hedge a word war, because no one could come between me and my baby's dad.

She caught my drift but then raised her brow, seeming to be caught off guard. "Dang, Z-gurl. Me sorry, but why you get so sensitive now? We always kick it."

"I don't know. Maybe my hormones are all over the place. Either way, play it easy about my boo. He might not be the best nigga this city has to offer, but he's my family now."

"Fuck it! I can't take it anymore!" The Jamaican lady's random outburst silenced the room and drew everyone's attention her way, though her focus was set only on me. We were stating one another directly in the eyes. I knew there was something about her that I didn't like. I just didn't know the actual reason would be so bad.

"Hey, lady, you not disturb me shop. You get out and go." Kimmie snatched her mask off, stood up, and aggressively pointed at the door.

I'd seen all her movements out of my peripheral vision because I never took my eyes off the chick who'd called me out. "Whatchu want with me? You got a problem?" I cut over Kimmie, not wanting the girl to leave or address Kimmie before I got to find out what her beef was.

She rolled her eyes. "No, no, no. You're the one with the problem. I've been listening to your delusional ass make up stories since I got in here, and I've had it enough. You need to be real with yourself and everyone in here, honey. Renard is not your family anymore, and he never really was if you ask him how the story started and unfolded."

I cringed at hearing her call Nardo by his government name. If looks could kill, she would've dropped dead on the scene. I ain't bullshittin'. But since they couldn't, I had to do it with my bare hands.

"Don't move, bitch. I'm about to beat the weight off yo' bulky-shaped ass."

"No, Z! No fight in me shop." Kimmie was trying to hold me down by my ankles.

"Wow, you're such a feisty little rat. No wonder Renard doesn't want you," she hissed. "Maybe you should consider stepping your game up, because that baby you be calling about all day and night will not get him back. Maybe get some braids or something like that!"

The brazen ho had taken me to the limits. Fuck respecting Kimmie and her hood-zoned shop. It was on, and I was boiling with hate. "Kiss my ass!" I screamed loudly as I leaped in her direction, grabbing her by the throat. My hands were shaking as I gripped her neck as tightly as I could in an effort to snap her head off her body. I tried ramming her headfirst into the wall, but truth be told, the island bitch had a little strength to go with her slick mouth.

"No, no, no!" Kimmie kept excitedly shouting. "You two not fight in here! Break it up! Break it up right now!"

Kimmie was shrieking at the top of her lungs, but I blocked all of that out as me and my nemesis fell to the ground. I was on a mission to demolish this mystery homewrecking floozy by taking out her moderately cute face.

Reaching up, she tried to pry my now-strained hands from the grip around her neck, but my fury was too strong and my strength too much for my island competition. I was trying to strangle the breath out of her lungs. Finally getting some wits, she smacked me in the face.

"Get off of me." She barely got her words out because I was cutting off her oxygen.

I knew she had more bombs to drop but couldn't catch the air she needed to say them. I was now the predator, and she was the prey. Guess it doesn't pay off to run your mouth in the long run. I became more infuriated because her little bitch slap made my left cheek sting and burn.

"Bitches smack. True muthafuckas try bodying bitches."
I sent a punch into her face and blew her mouth out.
Blood squirted from her busted lips, which made me
want to send my fist into each one of her eyes and black
those muthafuckas too. That would be what she deserved
for side-eyeing me so cockily earlier. Homegirl was no
contest to me since I was used to boxing bitches out on
Linwood Avenue on my way home from Central High.
It was nothing to me and mine when it came to putting
uppity-acting bitches like her in their place.

"You two not fight in here! Break it up now. You two not
fight in here." Kimmie kept shouting, begging us to stop
tearing up her property. "Get off her, Z. Day-um. She not
worth it, Z. Nardo gonna have you fight a million girls.
Stop this and get up." Kimmie had no idea she was gonna
catch a hot one in her jaw if she didn't get her damn
hands off of me. In my world, you're either with me or
against me.

"Back the hell up, Kim." I threw my hand back to push
Kim back from me and ol' girl's space, then used the same
hand to snatch a bunch of braids out of the woman's
head. I was a savage with it. "Talk now, homewrecker.
I'm a gold-digging what?" I repeated, taunting the now
helpless woman. "Where's all that mouth at now?"

"Get up, honey. Not in shop, please. You tear my shit up,
you pay." Kimmie and her workers managed to separate
us two. Must've been an act of God.

I didn't care about Kimmie's damn shop. I was hot
like boiling water. Nobody fronted me off, period. "Keep
talking. Please, keep talking," I insistently begged the girl.
"Don't bitch up now."

"Oh, you've heard enough," she sarcastically whispered
as she got up off the floor, holding her neck. "Your eyes
need to do some watching." She wanted round two; yes, it
was clear. It would be my pleasure, I thought, revving up
to pounce back on her.

"Bitch, next time I see you, it won't be nothing friendly." I mocked her Jamaican accent as I victoriously waved a handful of braids that I'd ripped out by the roots.

"You may have won the battle, but the man will be mine," she promised before rushing out the door.

I tried going after her for my round two, but Kimmie and her Korean crew had me held back against the wall.

These little short, stocky muthafuckas really do have some muscle.

"Are you a'ight, Z?" Kimmie asked as she released me and her squad backed off, scattering like tiny work ants to get back to their wide-eyed customers.

"Yeah, that chick was nothing, and I'm waiting to see that ass again." Knowing I'd put on a helluva show for real, I wanted the word to spread like wildfire in the hood that Nardo's baby momma was not the one to be tested. "Let it be known that anyone fucking my man will be on the chopping block to be dealt with. You already know, stomped the fuck out." Feeling my ego, I was talking mad shit and waiting for the next brave soul to try me.

"Well, I'm glad for you, but next time you want to fight Nardo's ho, take shit outside. This me business," Kimmie fairly stated with attitude while looking around for any damages to her shop that she could charge my black ass for.

"Yup, Kimmie, you've got my word—if we make it that far," I fired back. After what just went down, I was not getting ready to apologize or explain why I'd lost my cool. If her gotta-have-gossip ass was not fishing for some entertainment, ol' girl wouldn't have had anything to comment on. "Now, about that pedicure . . ." I kept a brave front, walking to the chair so we could resume my much-needed rest and relaxation time.

Kimmie shook her head and started back on my pinky toe. Rain, sleet, snow, or a fist fight in the middle of her money, she was still going to manage to chase a dollar. Reaching over into my Gucci purse, I threw the braids I'd captured out of her head into it. Nardo would have some serious questions to answer when I got home. As the clock ticked, I was beyond anxious to find out who I'd just beat down in the name of love.

CHAPTER FOUR

Zaria

Though I'd gotten the best of ol' girl and walked out of the nail salon the winner of the war, the victory didn't stop the pain my heart was feeling. The truth was in my face—again. I had been faithful, loyal, and stupid to Nardo's lies. It had been hard as hell to keep a straight face while Kimmie finished my pedicure. And now that I was gone, I knew those heifers were talking about me like clowns, and Kimmie was the circus leader. I didn't blame them for being entertained, however. It was not like me and Nardo's jump-off hadn't given them a helluva show.

The nail shop wasn't too far from my mom's crib so, I drove past to make sure everything looked straight on the outside, then swooped down on my homeboy. Growing up, Deuce and I used to call each other brother and sister, though we did not have the same blood running through our veins or DNA in our genes. Deuce is, was, and would always be my family, because he had always been loyal. That was more than I could say for the man—and I used that word loosely to describe Nardo right about now—I chose to start a family with. After all the manipulation and lies, I did not know if I was more upset with him or myself.

"Bro!" I pulled up, yelling out of the window. "Come kick it with yo' sis for a sec."

He was smiling hard, happy to see me, until he got into the car. "Damn, sis. What happened to you?" he questioned me, concerned because I was sweating and my appearance was disheveled. "Don't tell me that ho-ass nigga put his hands on you. Do I need to go strap up?" Deuce had always been my protector, beating up bullies for me before I learned how to.

He did not like Nardo, and not because they both hustled dope in the streets. Deuce was my go-to guy whenever I needed a male's perspective. In other words, he was extremely versed on the bullshit I'd been tolerating out of my baby daddy. He had also been the most vocal person in telling me to dead my relationship with Nardo.

"Naw, he didn't put his hands on me, but his ho-ass side chick did." I proceeded to tell him about what happened at the nail shop.

"You're gonna have to calm all that ra-ra bullshit down, Z. For real. What are you gonna do if you're out with Cid and a bitch tries you?"

"Hit her over the head with Cidney on my hip," I joked, but I knew what Deuce was getting at. He didn't want his niece targeted or to become a casualty behind some bullshit her mother and father couldn't get right.

Deuce tipped the ash off his blunt outside of my window and then responded to my comment like he'd just had an epiphany. "Yo' ass is just as crazy as Auntie is," he said, referring to my mother as his aunt, just as I referred to his mom as mine. "And Cidney is gonna be just as crazy as the both of you."

"Yup, it's embedded in her genes." I reached over and put my hand out for the blunt. I was not a smoker, but I did want to take a few puffs.

"I don't know why you're so scared of being without that nigga, though. It ain't like you and Cidney will be out here alone if you leave him. You know I'm here." Deuce sounded offended.

"I'm not scared. I just want my family." My voice drifted off. "And on our good days, I swear it feels like Nardo wants our family too."

"Why? 'Cause that nigga comes over with some carryut and watches movies with you on the couch before fuckin'? Naw, that doesn't mean he wants his family, and I know you don't believe that bullshit." Deuce was not sugar-coating the truth. "It doesn't take nothing for that man to throw some money at you and my niece and fall through there every couple of days with some empty promises."

I sat back, catching a contact and listening to him advise me for about fifteen minutes. I'd swooped down on him for a male's perspective and ended up getting angrier. The truth most definitely hurt.

"Can you roll me up a blunt to smoke for later? I'm sure I'm gonna need it after I get home and confront Nardo."

He shook his head while digging in his pocket for his stash of baggies. Deuce sold marijuana as a hustle and worked at a factory through a temporary service part-time. "Yo' ass kill me, having a habit but can't support it."

"Yeah, whatever. It's not a habit. It's a soother."

"I see you make it a habit to tell yourself whatever you need to hear to get through the struggle."

His honesty hit my heart. "Just for you trying to be funny, roll me up two."

I slowly drove into the driveway of my two-story brick home, wondering how I was going to play my position with Nardo. At the end of the day, I heard every single word that Deuce had schooled me with, and I understood that Nardo was playing me. Hell, I didn't need Deuce to tell me that. I was sick to my stomach over being in love and loyal to the lies Nardo had been keeping me line with.

As I vindictively stared at his car, I couldn't believe he had the balls to mess around with some Jamaican trash. Each time he stepped out on me, my hood celebrity status deteriorated. Nardo had to pay for playing me to the left, and I had to get my situation straight quick. Zaria was not getting ready to go down like that.

Turning the key and slowly opening the door, I tiptoed onto the gray-and-black marble floor in my disposable pedicure slippers. I knew Nardo wouldn't hear me with them on.

I heard a movie playing on the television, but no other movement or sound in the house. Slowly creeping down the short hallway, I cautiously peeped around the corner and saw Nardo stretched out on the couch and our baby girl across the room in her bouncer. Deuce's opinion of Nardo wanting to be a family man was right. Instead of bonding with Cidney, maybe having her across his chest, he was allowing the television to soothe her. Nardo was acting like a babysitter rather than her father.

Out the corner of my eye, I caught a glimpse of his cell phone on the coffee table, and my curiosity was piqued. It had been a while since I'd gone through it, but today would either be my luckiest or most dreadful time of them all. Butterflies were swarming around in my stomach as I slid his phone from inside the holster. That was my sign from God to stop because my feelings were about to get hurt, but of course, I couldn't fight the urge to snoop. I wanted to see what he'd been up to. I wanted to see if there was some truth behind ol' girl's claims of being his future and me being his past. I wanted to see how much dirt he'd done so I could know how many times I'd have to put my foot off into ol' girl's Jamaican behind.

Let me see. My curiosity led my movements.

Quickly scrolling through his call log and text messages, all I saw was female names and a bunch of nicknames that I knew belonged to females. Instead of playing with Cidney, he'd been chit-chatting all fucking day with one heifer after the next. Whoever this Spice character was, she got more phone time than me. Judging from the call durations, I could see that these two were constant phone friends, having conversations from fifteen minutes to an hour. Yeah, so off rip, me and this Spice chick had problems.

It was hard to keep my cool, 'cause I was ready to clown. Noticing Cidney was starting to squirm, I had to make my Inspector Gadget search move a little faster. Taking a mental note of Spice's number, I hurriedly scrolled to his photo gallery.

Damn, it gots to be more than this. There was no way I could be coming up so dry. Ol' girl had too much of an opinion to just be some one-night hood jump-off.

Going through the picture gallery left me privy to what pieces of ass he was willing to hit. Never once did I see a picture of me or Cid, besides the ones I'd sent in his text messages. Me or mine didn't mean enough to be saved. Duly noted.

Get the fuck out of here. This nigga got me fucked up. Yeah, it was on and time to get turned up. I hadn't come up empty-handed, and this trifling nigga had some explaining to do.

"What the fuck is this bullshit?" I started my ghetto-style interrogation, stomping into the living room. "Nardo, get yo' stinking ass off my couch, nigga, and answer me!" I yelled as loud as I could.

Standing firm in his face, I refused to be ignored or back down. It took him a second to wake up and recognize what was going on and that I had his phone gripped tightly in the palm of my hand.

"Z, you don't pay no fucking bills, so don't be going through what don't belong to yo' ass." He tried ignoring my questions, snatching for his phone. "And on top of all that, where in the hell have you been?"

"I'm the one asking the questions, Nardo. Who is this tack-head heffa? And please don't say this is your bastard child," I suggested, frantically pacing the floor.

This picture had me beyond heated. I hadn't even revealed to him the events that jumped off earlier. Seeing the same chick's twisted face in his gallery with the ugliest monkey kid I'd ever seen on her hip was about to get a hard, inanimate object smashed upside his big damn head. He'd fucked with the wrong one.

"Zaria, I'm trying to keep my cool," Nardo insisted while lacing up his shoes. "So, don't ask me another question about what's in my phone. And P.S., her child is innocent and doesn't have anything to do with it. Just like Cid," he felt the need to remind me. Standing up, shaking the wrinkles from his clothes, he dismissed my hurt emotions and mixed feelings.

"You've gotta be kidding me. Is this for real? Are you sitting up in my freaking house, in my face, taking up for that whore and her child?" My hands were posted on my hips, and I was ready to charge toward his ungrateful behind. I'd given him the world. I'd given him all of me. Yes, indeed, he owed me answers.

Nardo rushed me before I could blink. "I'm tired of you, Zaria. Now, I asked you nicely, and we both know I'm not the type of nigga that's into asking twice," he threatened, pinning my body up against the wall.

"Back the hell up, Nardo, and get your dirty hands off me. They probably were all over that mangy heffa." I twisted my face and lips. Struggling to free myself from his strong grip, I could hear Cidney becoming fussy.

"Stay in your damn place, Zaria. I've had more than

enough of your ratchet-acting ass. She's a better woman than you anyway," he taunted me, shoving me harder into the wall, causing a mirror to fall. As the glass shattered loudly across the floor, both me and the baby yelled. What was next?

"Get the fuck out, nigga! Get the fuck on to her then!" Emotion-driven, I dug my freshly manicured nails into his back and face. Ducking and dodging, he only took a few scratches.

"Yeah, okay. Baby, you can believe I was planning to do that anyway. You've been replaced a long time ago. I was just trying to spare your feelings and be there for Cid, but to hell with all this drama," he gloated, releasing my frame, acting as if he was entitled to belittle me.

His words were starting to hurt, but I had no choice but to accept them. With everything out in the open, I now knew where he'd been laying his head when he wouldn't come here or would ignore my calls— with that ape and her repulsive offspring. He didn't need to be taking care of someone else's child when he had ours to raise. He was giving her the family I so desperately wanted.

"Humph, is that right? Well, Nardo, if you want to leave, then get the fuck on, fool. Ain't no bitches around here stopping ya! I'm tired of smelling yo' stank nuts anyway. Plenty of ballers want me," I barked, angry and hurt that he was being so damn irrational and evil.

"Come on now, Zaria, with the headache. The shit is played out, and it's over. I quit. My patience has been worn thin with you, and that's why I haven't been trying to be in your pathetic presence anyway. If another dude wants yo' good-begging, baby-momma-tainted ass, then fly the fucking coop. I made yo' gutter ass into a gold star anyway. It's nothing! I'm a boss!"

Out of breath from his insults, I didn't even know what to say to him. I was tired and confused. Here I was raising his child, his first-born no less, and he was not even trying to give me enough respect to be referred to as the mother of his child. Instead, I was his baby momma; a good-begging gutter one at that!

"Sweetie, why can't we just try and be a family? I'm all insecure and shit because you run out of here never giving me confirmation that you love me," I pleaded with tears burning in my eyes, grasping at straws. As I realized that Spice had been right and I was getting ready to lose out on everything I worked so long for with him, my world started to crumble.

"Family?" He said the word like it was foreign to him. "Bitch, fuck family! I don't even know if Cidney is mine," he bellowed out of his mouth, making me lose all compassion and hope.

I had never witnessed so much anger in his eyes, and I knew at that moment it was truly my harsh reality that he was done with me once and for all. I was devastated. Nardo had never repeated what the streets said about Cidney not being his, and now it had come to him throwing it in my face. I had run out of ways to keep him coming back to me.

It was not shit I could say about nothing because I had no plans on explaining the paternity of my child. He knew how scummy we got down, never once using a rubber. If he wanted to listen to the grimy streets, then so be it. My child's paternity didn't have to be no muthafuckin' twisted mystery like he was making it. All boss niggas know about doing sneak swab DNA tests, so get a Q-tip and push on!

"So, now it's fuck family, huh, Nardo? You'd rather walk out on our years and be with her?" I quizzed with a shaky voice, giving him the privilege and opportunity to stick the knife even deeper.

"She has a name, and it's Spice." He possessed a coldly condescending tone, staring directly through me.

My hurt feelings meant nothing to him, and that was crystal clear. He'd called Spice at my house, sitting with our daughter, disrespecting the make-believe family I though we shared. And even though he knew I'd pop the lock on his phone at any free moment, Nardo still kept several pictures of the other life he was living with her.

"Dude, you're really taking this shit too far." I rolled my eyes, having a flashback of the beatdown I'd put on his pet silverback gorilla.

"You're absolutely right. I should've been gotten rid of your miserable ass. Knocking you up was definitely taking it too far."

"Well, you better get on out of here then, Nardo," I bravely commanded, gritting my teeth and nodding my head. Fuck going through another second of his verbal thrashing. Nardo may not have given two sweet fucks about my loyalty or his daughter, but I did. I refused to let his ungrateful behind see me sweat another day. No longer did I need Renard or his sympathy. I needed revenge.

"Oh, yeah. Before you go—"

"What? What is it? What the fuck is it now? I know yo' ass ain't about to ask for a muthafucking thang," He cut me off, getting gutter and tough. His tone fueled my hate for him even more.

"I ain't about to ask you for shit, boo. Believe that. Just make sure you get those tacky-ass braids out of my purse." I devilishly smiled, rubbing Cidney's back. "Yeah, nigga, now who got one up? I tagged that bitch at Kimmie's for running her mouth. And just for a heads up, it ain't over!" Now brazen and feeling myself, I was talking mad shit.

Walking toward the door, he pulled out the handful of trophy braids from my purse and nonchalantly tossed them onto the marble floor. His mug was torn up because he'd been caught in his web of deceit, and I'd molly-whopped his lover.

"I wouldn't lay another finger on Spice if I were you, Zaria," he called himself warning me.

"I ain't worried about you or that bum bitch. G'on and do you, Nardo." I threw my hand up and shooed him.

He snickered like he was amused. "I ain't never needed your permission to do me, baby girl. Trust and believe that." His cockiness broke my ego. "I'll see you around."

Knowing he couldn't hear me, I rocked back and forth, trying soothe our li'l baby and ease the rage burning inside of me to run outside and clown on his ass. Hearing his engine start, I jumped up and looked out the window right as he was burning rubber out of the driveway. "Daddy will be back, baby." I kissed Cidney and hoped I wasn't lying.

CHAPTER FIVE

Nardo

I walked out of Zaria's place knowing I'd hurt her badly, but for some reason, I didn't feel much remorse. She knew what type of man I was when she started messing around with me. It was her best friend Melanie who she stole me from. Living up to her reputation as an opportunist, she respected no loyalty when it came to checking for me. With me being a roughneck nigga carrying heavy clout in the streets, I lived wild and reckless, and she was in love with the guaranteed money. But karma is a muthafucka, and rest assured, karma is meant to go around. So, I guess it was my turn to serve Zaria hers.

Feeling my phone vibrate, I looked down to see Spice had texted a multi-media message, cursing Zaria's existence and me at the same time. There were no hard feelings on my end toward her at this point. Spice had every reason to turn up on me. However, it was not in my DNA to take cops. It was what it was, and she knew how messy shit could get when baby mommas were involved.

Real talk, Spice probably was not expecting the ghetto girl fist job Z had put onto her high-class behind. But that's what she deserved for being in Zaria's nail shop in the first place. It's like she caught what she had coming. Her sore scalp and head were reasons to learn a lesson: don't look for trouble and then throw a pity party. Spice had stepped out of line by searching for beef and creating one between me and mine. This whole chain of events was nothing but a reminder that I needed to get my shit balanced and together with these chicks quick.

Not being one to leave a trail of incriminating text messages, I hit CALL and waited to be connected instead of responding to her typed rants. None of this bullshit would've been going down had she fallen back and played the position I'd directed for her. But naw, just like Zaria had bossed up on Melanie, Spice couldn't resist the urge to claim what she felt was rightfully hers.

"So, I know that low-class baby momma of yours told you her version." She answered the phone with much expected attitude.

"Not really. I mean, from what I do know, yo' ass should not have been anywhere near where Zaria gets her nails done. That is the truth pill you need to swallow." I was not getting ready to cut Spice any slack or baby her into thinking she didn't deserve consequences.

"Whatever," she said, smacking her teeth, not wanting to admit the truth. "Look, I'm not about that ghetto life she apparently likes to live, and you can trust I had no intentions of scrapping it up with the little skeezer. Kimmie is in every hair and nail promotional magazine throughout metro-Detroit. Who knew I'd run into yo' girl?" Spice must've taken my street diploma for dumbness, but I was not playing along.

"Kill that lying shit, Spice. I ain't with it." In all seriousness, I was starting to need a break from her nagging ways too. Thank God I kept a crib of my own.

"You're gonna believe what you want anyway. I'm just tired of playing the backfield to someone so beneath me. I've given up too much for you. I've shown my loyalty."

"A'ight, ma. Chill on that. We already know you are one hundred for a nigga. You won't let me live that shit down or forget it." I was exhausted from repeatedly hearing her throw it up in my face. No matter what issues and drama Spice was having with her peeps, she was not getting ready to strong-arm me into the corner about how I lived my life. "You really need to be easy. I already look out for you and li'l man like he is my own, and I've already started to get my baby moms in order. You are doing too much trying to flaunt and throw it in her face, making shit more complicated for me," I scolded her.

"If you say so, Renard. But please do not make me look like a fool to my father," she pleaded. "When are you coming home? Li'l man has been asking about you."

"I've got business in the streets. Nothing has changed about that. Pop a Motrin and tell my li'l homie I'll check for him in a few."

"Okay. I love you."

"Yeah, that's real," I responded to her affection, refusing to let those three heavy words give Spice more of a reason to try to put me on a leash. "I promise you that I will be home tonight, so cool out."

"Sure, Renard. We will be here waiting on you, as usual." She hung up, apparently salty that I had not shown love back. Women nowadays have too much nerve and audacity.

Merging onto the entrance ramp of the John C. Lodge Freeway, I set the cruise control to fifty-five miles per hour and adjusted my mirrors to keep an eye out for the State boys. Their troopers had been out targeting speeders all week, and riding dirty with no license, I was not trying to get caught up in the sting.

Connecting my phone to the car's audio system, I voice-dialed Izzi and waited on him to answer.

"What up, guy? Are you headed to the block or what?"

"Man, you will never believe the straight bullshit that popped off today. The baby momma and Spice scrapped it up at the nail shop earlier, and Zaria had the nerve to come home bossing up on me." I spilled my guts to Izzi.

"Dude, you lying. Straight up?"

"Naw, man. But I wish I was. You already know I was not trying to get caught up the between the two of their crazy asses."

"Yo' mouth say that, but yo' dick been making different decisions." Izzi spoke in that I-told-you-this-would-happen tone.

"To make matters even worse, though, Zaria went through my phone and saw pictures of the kid." I shook my head, still in disbelief. "She straight clowned."

"Hell yeah! Why wouldn't she go straight nuts on yo' ass, man? I been trying to tell yo' ass to quit playing mind games with these chicks. Just pick one. But naw, you wanna be an ol' Rico Suave type nigga." He laughed, putting me on front street.

"Aw, man, fuck you, dude! I put her back in check hella quick and got Spice waiting on a nigga to pull up. My game is tighter than tight, bro, so you ain't even gotta worry." Rubbing at my goatee, I knew Izzi was being real, but nobody liked hearing when they were dead wrong.

"Who do you think you're fooling? Whether you put Zaria in check or got ol' girl swinging from your nut sac, you'll be back over there next week like ain't shit popped off." He continued to go hard. "Enough on your sob story, nigga. Business grinding, and you caking."

"I'm on the e-way, chief. Be cool."

"But that ain't exchanging packages or picking up paper, you feel me? You letting them broads fuck yo' moves up!" Izzi was taking his right-hand man title to the head. "But that's on you. Don't let me motivate your change. I'm out to murder these fools on a dice game. Pull up. We out here."

"Oh, you can believe I'm about to pull up, taking all you jokers' stacks," I joked with him, but he'd rubbed me the wrong way. Izzi was starting to get on my bad side. For some reason, I was catching a serious itch from his vibe, and something didn't sit right. I never allowed people to speak out of term too long, whatever the case might be, and he was doing it a little too much for me. My plan was to put a stop to that disrespect and quick.

The block was on fire. Fiends and goons were posted up in front of every abandoned house and vacant lot on the poorly maintained block. Izzi and our hired street crew had the corner swarmed with hoodlums and hot hoes, street gambling and socializing. Bringing heat and attention to the otherwise uneventful block, I parallel parked my ride, careful not to scratch the rims.

"Open this door up, nigga."

I looked over to see a ratchet-acting Melanie tapping on my window. *Damn, this ain't my day at all.*

"Yo, what up?" I rolled the window down halfway.

"Um, I'm trying to find out. Can you open the door?" she asked, pulling up on the door handle. "And don't be rolling the window down on me like I'm a custo."

With offense in her voice, hesitation was in my moves. Even though I hit the automatic lock and allowed her to slide into my passenger's seat, deep down inside I knew my messy ex couldn't be trusted.

"So, where have you been at all day?" Melanie turned in her seat, staring at me. I gave her the bitch-don't-question-me look, so she continued on to explain, "Me and my girls been over here barbecuing over at the park. I've been checking for you to see if you wanted a plate."

"Yeah, you can fix a nigga a healthy portion, ma." I had to give Melanie her props. Cooking was her strong suit, keeping a nigga full.

"Okay, I got you on that. But what's up with us? I've been thinking about you lately and how you used to feel up inside me."

Her pleas weren't falling on deaf ears. Feeling my dick rise in my boxers, I wished that Mel was not so fuckin' ill-bred. The possibility of having my cake and eating it too was sitting wide-legged right next to me, waiting on a quick ho feel-up, but I had to make a better judgment call. I wouldn't have had the Magnum all the way down my shaft before she'd be blabbing to her loudmouthed friends, not learning from Zaria's double-crossing. Ain't nobody had time for the extra drama Mel would bring, especially with Spice showing up and showing out unexpectedly.

"Girl, chill the fuck out with yo' needy ass. Don't keep stalking me for no dick. When I want it, I'll check for you—trust." I dismissed all conversation.

"Hold on. Wait a second. So, it's like that now? After all the history we have with each other, you just gon' kick me out yo' ride, nigga? I was down with your ass when you couldn't carry me on shit but those raggedy-ass handlebars." She brought a smile to my face, bringing back the old hustle-boy memories. I'd come a long way from being the watch boy working for sneakers.

"Ha! Girl, you tripping. I remember that squeaky piece of shit." Stopping in mid-step getting out of my car, Mel had taken me back down memory lane. "But we've come a long way since then, Mellie-Mel, and there's no going back." I knew my words were getting underneath her skin. Unlike Zaria and Spice, of course, Melanie was there for it all, making us have a natural bond. In her case, shit got old, and she got played. I didn't need any extra temptation from her.

"Dang, Nardo, I just missed having you around. We had fun, that's all. I just missed you," she whined with regret in her voice for stepping to my car at all.

***

was at my mom's, so it was time to do me. I
onably needed some time out, partying to get
my mind and get my spirits back on point. Still
banging body post carrying Cid's eight-pound
r nine months, I couldn't wait to get back heavy
eets of Detroit. With my baby daddy claiming
of the picture, getting back into action would
ss, and all a bitch had to do was appear on the

a long, hot bath with aromatherapy candles,
nagining my life was perfect to soothe my
verything inside of me was tense and worked
ng to release my rage sooner than later on all
volved, I sipped on the chilled glass of wine,
buzz.

clothes from all the dresser drawers and off
ngers, tearing up my small room for something
ar. I had to have all eyes on me, especially since
hem to run back and tell my baby daddy they'd
aying. I wanted him jealous and in his feelings
ge. Nardo was notorious for playing a role of
a fuck when it came to me, but it was not no
shit bricks on sight knowing I was flaunting
around Motown. Good for him, though—that
n.

hoosing a soft pink-and-white maxi skirt with
bow top, I slid them over my butter-smooth
ing certain all assets popped. I'd considered
ssed, not having stretch marks or a kangaroo
cessorizing with a diamond cross pendant,
ngs, and the iced-out ring Nardo gave me as a
rying his firstborn seed, everything appeared
ss.

"Well, keep on missing me, and don't slam my car door getting out." I cut her off completely, stepping out to join my crew.

Izzi never stopped watching with a grim face and folded arms as me and Melanie conversed. For this nigga to be out here reckless, helping to bring heat to the block, he sure was trying to oversee me like a boss.

"What up, playa?" I gave Izzi dap as he scooped up his winnings and threw his arm around my shoulder. "Let's do this deal."

CHAP

Z

Spice had no heavenly
Nardo had crossed me bi
severe penalty. Being a n
I felt Spice trying to lato
ticket that was Nardo, b
helluva fight on her han
come-up of another chic
set my stalk mission into

Never hearing of a f
searched on all the socia
Spice. Nowadays, it's ea
rests their head or freque
snitches, and these soci
nition. Fuck helping a ni
every possible GPS locat
with a password to turn

Having come up with
and followed her for fut
though. Spice left her p
application gave away
Spice stayed in Novi, M
drive from my house, bu
down. She could have
for all I cared. My so-
second-round ass-whoo

Cid
unque
Nardo
having
behind
in the
to be c
be effo
scene.

Taki
I tried
nerves.
up. Wa
parties
chasing

I toss
all the h
sexy to
I wanted
seen me
for a ch
not givir
secret he
"his" ass
was the p

Finally
matching
skin, ma
myself bl
pouch. A
hoop earr
gift for c
to be flaw

"Well, keep on missing me, and don't slam my car door getting out." I cut her off completely, stepping out to join my crew.

Izzi never stopped watching with a grim face and folded arms as me and Melanie conversed. For this nigga to be out here reckless, helping to bring heat to the block, he sure was trying to oversee me like a boss.

"What up, playa?" I gave Izzi dap as he scooped up his winnings and threw his arm around my shoulder. "Let's do this deal."

CHAPTER SIX

Zaria

Spice had no heavenly idea who she was dealing with. Nardo had crossed me big time and was going to pay a severe penalty. Being a real woman, I could admit that I felt Spice trying to latch onto her seven-course meal ticket that was Nardo, but she was about to have one helluva fight on her hands. I was not interested in the come-up of another chick. After putting in her swing, I set my stalk mission into full effect.

Never hearing of a female with that nickname, I searched on all the social sites for any possible leads to Spice. Nowadays, it's easy to find out where a person rests their head or frequents the most. Smart phones are snitches, and these social videos help with voice recognition. Fuck helping a nigga build a case on me. I turned every possible GPS locater and tracker on my phone off with a password to turn on.

Having come up with a few hits, I made a fake page and followed her for future reference. It was not needed, though. Spice left her page public, and her preloaded application gave away her direct, pinpointed location. Spice stayed in Novi, Michigan. Damn, that would be a drive from my house, but fuck the dumb shit, it was going down. She could have stayed in Boon Foo Foo, Egypt for all I cared. My so-called replacement was due the second-round ass-whooping fate would deal her ass.

***

Cidney was at my mom's, so it was time to do me. I unquestionably needed some time out, partying to get Nardo off my mind and get my spirits back on point. Still having a banging body post carrying Cid's eight-pound behind for nine months, I couldn't wait to get back heavy in the streets of Detroit. With my baby daddy claiming to be out of the picture, getting back into action would be effortless, and all a bitch had to do was appear on the scene.

Taking a long, hot bath with aromatherapy candles, I tried imagining my life was perfect to soothe my nerves. Everything inside of me was tense and worked up. Wanting to release my rage sooner than later on all parties involved, I sipped on the chilled glass of wine, chasing a buzz.

I tossed clothes from all the dresser drawers and off all the hangers, tearing up my small room for something sexy to wear. I had to have all eyes on me, especially since I wanted them to run back and tell my baby daddy they'd seen me slaying. I wanted him jealous and in his feelings for a change. Nardo was notorious for playing a role of not giving a fuck when it came to me, but it was not no secret he'd shit bricks on sight knowing I was flaunting "his" ass all around Motown. Good for him, though—that was the plan.

Finally choosing a soft pink-and-white maxi skirt with matching bow top, I slid them over my butter-smooth skin, making certain all assets popped. I'd considered myself blessed, not having stretch marks or a kangaroo pouch. Accessorizing with a diamond cross pendant, hoop earrings, and the iced-out ring Nardo gave me as a gift for carrying his firstborn seed, everything appeared to be flawless.

Stepping in front of the mirror to check out my oh-so-fine reflection, I immediately knew my shit was on point. After unwrapping my hair and making sure each curl flowed perfectly, I generously applied a coat of Ka'oir Capricorn lipstick and high-popping gloss. Strapping on a pair of white six-inch studded stiletto sandals, seeing my curvaceous behind rise up screaming for attention, I knew tonight was going to be my comeback on the real. Nothing or no one could stop my shine. Grabbing my keys and Louis Vuitton, making sure none of Spice's tacky braids were left behind, I was out the door in no time, eager to be reintroduced into downtown party life.

Hitting the freeway, I arrived downtown in record time. Pulling my deep cherry red Camaro into the valet line for Floods, I peeped the usual high-rollers and big-spenders were in packs, with loud music and flashy cars. Knowing damn near everyone posted in and around the popular Detroit city bar and grille, every move I made would be calculated because a bitch would be watched. Keeping my windows rolled up and Big Sean's album on low, I bobbed my head and kept it pretty, knowing even the least obvious hater was watching. Even on my worst day I'd stunt on these hoes, and since I was feeling myself, they were about to get murdered.

"Hey, honey, here's your ticket." The valet attendant opened my door with a wide smile. Not being reserved, he checked me out from head to toe.

Stretching one leg out slowly to tease the haters, I replied, "Thank you." I smiled but was careful not to flirt. Being that he parked cars for pay, he was not my type. So, giving him more than just an eyeful was not worth it. When he pulled my car off toward the reserved section, I marched out solo, making my way past the long line, knowing he'd better not scratch my ride.

Shit, I wish I would think I'm about to join these broke bitches in line.

Standing for entry? Me? Never! It was nothing to jump the ropes, bypassing these nobodies. Being extra cool with the bouncers from my party-all-the-time days, I was not surprised that they held the door open for my entrance. Mission fucking accomplished. Every cluck-cluck left behind in my arrogance was breaking their necks and rolling their eyes. I was not concerned with them no-ranking hoes. My mind was set on revenge against Nardo. Forget partying like a rock star; I was about to stunt like a superstar.

"What up, Z? You looking real good," one of the bouncers remarked as I strolled in the crowded club. He was one of the brothers I used to kick it with until Nardo upgraded me.

"Thanks, sweetheart." I giggled, slightly flirting with him. "But you know me. I ain't never missing a beat."

"You're right about that. Yo' man should've tied you up tighter!" he shouted out, acting like Nardo wouldn't have stomped his ass for even questioning his gangsta.

Giving him a half fake-ass smile, I barely laughed at his comment. I had to watch my words wisely. All eyes were on us, and I didn't want the wrong word to get back to Nardo. This guy was far from on my radar. "I need VIP. You know I can't do it any less."

"There was no doubt in my mind." He stumbled over his words while placing the paper strip around my tiny wrist. "And before you leave, holla at yo' man." He looked up at me with desperation in his eyes.

"You know it, playa."

Hell naw, I didn't have any intention of hooking up with him later, or any other day for that matter. But my ticket inside was free, so what the hell. Making a beeline toward the second bar in the back room and finding a stool, I sat down, ordering a Grey Goose with cranberry juice. The club was packed with all breeds from high rollers to gutter hoes. The pool tables were full, and the dance floor was filled to capacity. Sipping on my drink, letting the sounds take over my body, I tried picking up the eight-count steps the hustlers were throwing down on.

Guys were approaching me left and right, and I was giving them all a little attention too. Well, just enough to take notice of the price of their shoes. My moms always taught me you could judge a true playa by his shoe game. Anyhow, when the Ballroom Hustle came on, finally a step I'd mastered, I jumped off the stool and joined the dancers. I can't even lie; the drink had me feeling on point, and since I was not nursing Cid, I was ready for round two.

Every set of eyes were definitely on me, and that was a good thing. I'd dropped off the face of the earth going through pregnancy and being under Nardo's thumb. Especially taking notice of one of his street hustlers in the corner, I thought twice about going to shake my ass on him.

Hmm, I should give them a show.

I moved swiftly off the floor and toward the stalking bouncer whose eyes lit up when he realized I was heading in his direction. He grabbed my perfect body into a big bear hug and started feeling all over my booty, kissing on my neck. Real talk, the shit was grossing me out, but I knew Nardo would know soon that his baby momma was back on the prowl.

Melanie

Being dressed to impress with the most revealing outfit Rainbows had to offer, I held my ground in line, scoping the scene, hoping to see Nardo swerve up. When Zaria's shiny red Camaro bent the corner, my stomach dropped, and jealousy reared her ugly head.

Damn, this bitch is always killing my vibe.

Not being able to keep my eyes off the whip intended for me, my hatred for the back-stabbing bitch I once called my best friend grew. I wanted to—naw, I needed to get back at her for double-crossing me.

I had to admit Zaria had her A-game on and was looking all right, especially just having a baby and all, but she was still trifling. As she got out of the car and started walking past everybody in line as if we were supposed to bow down to her, getting revenge sooner than later was a must! Fighting back the urge to reach out and smack the taste from her mouth, I watched with envy as Zaria switched and floated right past me.

That rotten bitch. I know she saw me and flossed extra hard. Fuck her. It was everything in my power not to trip her stanking, man-stealing behind.

"Hold my spot down in line. I'll be right back," I announced to my clique. Too caught up in their own quests on pulling a meal ticket, they nodded nonchalantly, never missing a beat. I couldn't blame them for their thirst, however; mine was real too.

Zaria was too caught up in her popularity parade to notice me walk right past her toward the valet's reserved section. Waiting on the attendant to lock and leave her car, I snuck in behind him, pulling out my handy box-blade. Not choosing to go out with revenge the traditional way by fucking up her paint job, I began to unscrew the license plate from its place, making sure to stay concealed from oncoming traffic.

Since Zaria's car was backed in, giving me the perfect dark place to conduct my business, I had the plate off and tossed in the nearest dumpster within sixty seconds flat. Being from the hood, being a quick sneak was my craft. Being that it was a Saturday night in the D, the hot boys were out heavy, looking for drunk and illegal drivers. I'd just made sure my nemesis would stick out on their radar for sure!

Going unnoticed, I popped back into line. We'd inched up and were closer to the entrance. Even though I felt a little gratification for the sheist I'd just pulled off, I was anxious to get into Floods and make my presence known. Me and Zaria had not had a real chance to cross paths, but I wanted the ground underneath her feet to rattle at the sight of me.

CHAPTER SEVEN

Nardo

"So, are you ready to floss on these broke clowns and act a fool? We got one up on these sucka-ass lames in the streets. It's our time to shine." Izzi swerved in and out of lanes, recklessly coasting through traffic up Interstate 75. "I don't know about you, my dude, but I've been banking on that nigga shaking hands on our deal."

"Trust it's on. Once my manz pushes that weight our way, it's gonna be double-up time. I'm about to buy the bar out fa sho'." Mad love was getting ready to go down at the infamous Floods. Everyone in attendance was about to drink top-shelf and pop bottles with their crew.

"That's what I'm talking about. It's a fucking celebration for our team. Let's get it!" My right-hand man was lit, but still tilted back his personal bottle of 1738 like a skilled alcoholic.

"It's about to be a flock of groupies up in here tonight, bro. Are you talking 'bout adding to yo' roster?" Izzi questioned, sliding the now empty bottle underneath his car seat, exiting the Lafayette ramp. Greektown was banging, with bumper to bumper traffic heading to the casino, restaurants, or, like us, the nightlife.

"Naw, I'm straight. My starting line-up is going crazy, and a nigga ain't got time. I'm trying to be one hundred with Spice anyway. She's got class, and once her pops gets with the program, she'll have cash to hold a nigga down. Once I train that Jamaican ass on how to fall in line and put that mouth on ice, we'd be the next Jay and Bey, but in the drug game," I joked, pulling out my brush, getting my waves on point.

"Yeah, I hear you. But until then, I wouldn't advise you getting on baby momma's bad side. That shit can prove to be fatal, ya feel me?" Izzi played the role like he had kids or the problems I had with Zaria. Instead of buying diapers, his ass was pitching abortion campaigns to jump-offs he rammed in the hood.

"Nigga, please. Ain't nobody worried about Zaria's all-talk and no-action-having ass. Like I said, it's all about Spice now."

"A'ight, man, be easy. That's on you. As your ace, though, real talk: Zaria ain't no bum bitch. How are you gonna play your hand once cats try getting on?" He posed a question I'd never thought twice about.

Ol' boy caught me off guard with that one, knowing good and damn well I was not really ready for Zaria to dip out on a brother totally. I wanted that pussy a few more good times at least. Plus, needless to say, a brother had to admit the thought of someone else getting all of her love, devotion, and attention had me a little unnerved. Friend or not, I had to keep my front up. "Again, I ain't worried. Baby momma ain't about to put another player up, trust!"

"It only takes one real cat to show her the light." He called himself joking, but I held onto his words. Izzi was talking extremely bold to be speaking about my baby moms.

"Oh, yeah? Well, since you know word on the street, drop one that I'm lighting all contestants looking for a chance at that." I showed my hand, clearly not giving a fuck.

Izzi burst into laughter. "See, that's why yo' ass should quit talking shit. You ain't really ready to let Z go. Don't shoot the messenger, nigga." He realized how tightly cringed-up my face had become.

"I ain't got no beef with the messenger as long as he sends my word back with vengeance to the hood. Zaria is off limits."

"Ha! My nigga, you a nut! I feel you, though. If you ain't having her, no one else can. I got you, though. Trust and believe that."

His word was golden with me. Izzi's reputation was pristine, never going against the grain or giving me reason to question his loyalty. It was no question about it; hands down, Izzi would set them wanna-be-me-ass niggas straight. The only thing I was left thinking, however, was why didn't he do that in the first place? If I didn't know any better, I'd think he was trying to check for Zaria himself. Naw, he didn't want my chrome plate to his dome. Road dawg or not, shifty disloyal niggas got no respect.

Izzi was lit and loud as we walked through the club. Riding dirty in his cocaine-white Range Rover and 24-inch rims, the music was blasting "I'm so hood!" drawing attention and stares. Izzi had the porno playing on the back flat screens as a calling card he was on that tip. You could see the look of dismay on some chicks' faces, but some looked even harder.

Leaned all the way back in my chair, keeping a low profile, I left Izzi to stand out. Even though I was not trying to take no eye candy home, a nigga had to look! There were all type of females—tall, short, skinny, and fat—in line with their best outfits on. I might've been caught up in a lie; I might've been looking for an additional jump-off to fill the time while Zaria was on punishment. And even though my girl Spice was doing the Amazon on a nigga in bed, leaving me sprung doing double backs, variety was even better.

Of course, it was the usual hating bums who we'd shut down in the streets throwing hate, and the cats who were on our level trying to floss boss on some competition shit, but it was nothing to us, 'cause we stayed with the better hand. And once we laid our master plan down fully, our enemy list would grow.

"Hey, bro, don't take my shit over there in no alley. Park it over there by y'all booth." Izzi swung his door open, throwing commands to the attendant like he worked for him. My manz was looking bewildered. "Hey, you hear me right?" Izzi flashed two crumbled fifty-dollar bills in his face.

"Yup, I got you." He snatched and shoved the bills into his pocket. "I can take care of that most certainly."

Hopping out in a crisp pair of Mek jeans, black-and-red Detroit Made shit, and a pair of Jordan 4s, I was fresh off the block, hustling and grinding, ready to waste a pocket full of cash. Izzi kept his fit gutter with a pair of army fatigue cargo shorts, white tee, and Timberlands. A pigeon from the east side braided him up tight before he left the spot. We both made sure our reinforcement was tucked in the back of our pants. Fuck rules. Money made sure of that. I never parted from my piece. You'd never know when shit would pop off in the D.

The line was formed around the block, and the few dudes who thought their paper stretched far were pricing the ticket to get VIP status. We stood out on the scene, waiting for them to get their game right. Real bosses didn't have to question prices, 'cause they were too busy tossing cash and breezing in. These lame-ass niggas were wasting my time.

"So, we're walking in with you and Izzi, right?" Melanie's good-begging ass snuck up on me. "I knew you'd show up."

"Damn, you're like a stalker, yo! Where the fuck yo' ass just come from?" Izzi laughed loudly, putting my first ex on blast. Real talk, though, I felt him and wondered the same thing myself. Usually never being the one to be messy or involve himself with my chicks, I knew the liquor had him talking. Besides that, I wanted Mel's rat ass to go away.

"Man, whatever." She sucked her teeth, continuing on. "I ain't stalking, fool. Y'all just bent the corner. Me and my girls been in line for like thirty minutes already."

"Then keep wearing your soles sore. Me and my manz ain't about to walk in with no females." I dismissed her again.

"I'm so tired of your fat, funky ass acting like I ain't shit, Nardo. You was not saying that a few weeks ago, begging for some slob knob." She got loud, drawing even more attention my way. This heffa was bad for business, and her mouth only good if full.

"Girl, be gone with all that ra-ra shit. Take this twenty. Yo' girls are waiting." I pointed to her ratchet group of thirst mongers, wishing she'd raise up out my face. Dudes ahead of us had worked out some deal, finally clearing my path, but she was holding us up. She snatched the twenty but refused to move.

"Aw, nigga, you fooling tonight!" Izzi fronted her off even more. "It don't look like my manz is trying to fuck with you, sweetie. Save yourself the further embarrassment." My ace was on a roll as Melanie's face flushed red. For a split second, I felt sorry for her. She was not lying about our sexual escapades, but that was just it. I didn't want her for nothing more.

"Yeah, you're right. I got you, Nardo." As she stomped toward her girl, I watched her firm behind switch, wishing I could run my dick up and down its slit one last time.

"Damn, ol' girl got a fat ass, though!" Izzi rudely commented, watching her stand wide-legged on purpose, knowing I was still caught up staring. "No wonder you keep doing double backs. Let's get up in this club, nigga. You know it's slapping."

Melanie

I swear to God I don't know why I can't leave his ass alone.

I clutched my last twenty dollars in hopes that I didn't have to spend it on a drink to calm down. The last straw should have been him getting down with my girl then leaving me for her! Stomping back over to my clique, I was salty than a muthafucka and ready to light a fuse. Nardo couldn't help but to disrespect me. This nigga had some nerve and audacity leaving me to stand in line, holding brick walls up while he pranced in on big bills to party with bitches.

"Wow, Melanie, I guess Nardo really is done checking for you." My girl Rockie shook her head, holding back laughter. "I was just wondering when you planned on getting the point."

"Bitch, whatever! Nardo always be on some fake shit in front of people, but when we get behind closed doors, he stays with a mouth full of this cookie." I refused to hold back the truth, no matter how dumb it made me look.

"Well, in that case, you might want to have a serious sit-down conversation with that nigga on public etiquette. 'Cause right about now, you're looking real pathetic."

"Wow, just like that? We're supposed to be girls. That's how ya gonna cut into me?" I stepped back and eyed Rockie.

"I'm a real friend. A fake friend would fuck yo' man. Learn the difference," she proudly stated while dropping some knowledge in my ear.

Moving up to the front of the line, we were a few feet away from it all going down. With Nardo pulling another diss move on me, I'd neglected to inform him about Zaria being there. Once he got some liquor in his system, he'd be singing another tune, and I'd have his ass all in my face—trust! Nardo might've been playing me for a fool, but Zaria needed to know I ain't never stopped fucking with him on the side—not never one day.

CHAPTER EIGHT

Zaria

"Oh my God! I can't believe this nigga is here," I murmured and rolled my eyes to Nardo and Izzi walking through the front door like a couple of celebrities. I was irked to see him in the flesh but kinda turned on by how fine he looked. Chicks were on their heels like a pack of paparazzi as they strolled to the bar.

"Aw, naw, li'l momma. Don't stop dancing with a nigga just because that clown and his joker are here." The bouncer picked up on my all-of-a-sudden distant vibe and pulled me back into his space.

Backing up from the slow dance me and the bouncer were entangled in, I watched Izzi and Nardo stroll into the bar with less than a care in the world like a couple of celebrities. I wanted Nardo to hear about my presence, not actually see me. My original game plan would have to be sidetracked because I didn't know what he'd do, nor was I prepared for the embarrassment.

When the waitress came back past carrying a tray of Patrón shots, I slid her a twenty spot for two, wasting no time tipping them into my mouth. Trying to keep up with Izzi and Nardo from a distance was hard with guys pushing up on me from left and right. Too concerned over my baby daddy and if that ratchet trick Spice had accompanied him, I brushed off each dude with ease and kept my focus on Renard. Bet money, I was no longer in the mood for a parade of attention, or like Pac said, "All Eyez on Me." I couldn't risk Nardo peeping me out in the crowd.

The back booth of Floods was always reserved for big spenders and those willing to keep the party going all night. Izzi and Nardo had done just that, having hot box females glued by their sides. My attitude was on fire, peeping bottles of top-shelf liquor and Moët. Seeing Izzi make it rain on a few chicks as they twerked for attention had me livid.

It was itching me something awful to go over and blow the spot up, but I surprisingly held it in. Nardo couldn't be privy to knowing he had me twisted up, not having a good time on account of him. Even as he dipped off to the side, I still kept a keen-eye surveillance on him, watching his every move like a hawk.

Oh, no this bitch didn't. This nigga better not fucking show her no love.

Watching Melanie sneak back up on Nardo, hugging him from behind, I glared with ice-cold blood running through my veins.

"Hell fuckin naw," I muttered through gritted teeth, feeling my blood pressure rise. "It's about to be some shit," I all but yelled, making a few heads turn to see the commotion.

Watching Melanie grind her wide ass over Nardo made my stomach turn. She was working hard at seducing my baby daddy, and from the look of enjoyment on his face, her bold moves were working.

Nardo

The club was packed with half-dressed females. The youngins on the dance floor might as well have taken their shows to the strip club. It was ass everywhere. Fuck modesty. Me and Izzi made our way straight through the bar to our reserved VIP booth.

"Hey, honey, grab me and my boy a bottle of Cîroc each." It was time to get bent.

I don't pop Molly; I rock Tom Ford.

JAY-Z had the crowd jumping, and Melanie's yamp-ass episode outside hadn't killed my vibe at all. I was more than ready to party and get wasted with my manz.

"Yo, shit's on me tonight," Izzi boasted then slapped a few Benjamins on the counter. "I'm about to grab some ladies and get it to popping!"

When the waitress arrived with our bottles, I didn't wait on Izzi to throw them back. I needed to catch up with him.

"Hey, baby girl, grab me a shot of Patrón to get my high rolling." She rushed away eagerly after snatching Izzi's cash off the table and being told to keep the change.

My plan was to get fucked up and end up in a wet one by three in the morning sharp. Anything goes with the hoes that frequented Floods, and tonight, this was oh so true. Females were coming out of the woodwork, approaching me and Izzi. Word was strong that we had cash, so of course they wanted their fair share. Having the booth locked down, our private party was overflowing.

"Damn, here comes Mel and a flock of fools."

Izzi shook his head as the yesteryear cat I once banged on a daily basis approached me from behind. I didn't even care that one of Zaria's so-called friends, Kimmie, and her Korean crew took notice of me feeling all over Melanie. Them envious, bottom-barrel, slanted-eye whores just wanted to be next in line anyway.

She was hugging me, throwing the pussy my way again, and this time I didn't brush her off so quickly. With liquor running through my veins and a nigga's ego swollen from the amount of love chicks were throwing my way, Mel got in where shit fit in, and this happened to be the right time. The way she was grinding her plump ass on my dick had it rising to full attention.

I couldn't even front; her moves were turning me on. She drove a hard bargain and couldn't be denied. With me getting ready to lay the law down with Z, either she'd have to accept the new me or roll out. So, the alcohol had me thinking maybe I could still dig out Mel from time to time.

Mel turned around and started kissing all over my neck. Grabbing at my back with her nails, making sure to make those sex noises in my ear she used to make when I was inside of her, she was outright with her intent. "You taking me home with you tonight, Nardo?" she begged tenderly in my ear.

"And how do you know I'm not going home to Zaria later?"

"Just a feeling."

I'd known Melanie long enough to know her suddenly high-pitched voice meant she was up to something. Everyone knew she was channels two, four, and seven breaking news. Nobody needed to watch television when they had Miss Melanie on the scene. I had to come up with a quick solution to get both of us a quick fix. Her all-star performance had a nigga sweating, but there was no way I could pull an all-nighter with Spice already pissed. For sure, I was already on her bad side for not going over and personally checking on her after the nail shop smackdown.

"Breathe easy, baby girl. Let me grab Izzi's keys so we can get to the truck."

My plan was to bang Mel in my boy's ride at the Isle and get back inside the club. I was gonna tear her weave back so she'd look too raggedy to come back inside the club.

"Okay." She anxiously acted hard-up for the dick.

Zaria

Fuming, I watched Nardo and Melanie getting off on one another. That nigga had been fronting, acting like she was stalking him, dick riding, when all along he was feeding into it too. Feeling someone come up behind me and grab my waist, I twisted my body around with a quickness, ready to smack whoever this intruder was, when I stared directly into Izzi's big brown eyes.

Damn, busted, I thought.

"What the fuck?" I frowned up, still not removing his hands from my midsection.

"Be easy, Z. I see you sweating and shit." Izzi laughed. "Nardo don't know you're here. I peeped you when we first came in, but I ain't say shit. Dawg keeps telling me you and him a done deal and that he don't want you anymore, but you be hanging from his nut sac."

He pausing for a reaction, but I just rolled my eyes, shifting my weight with attitude.

"Anyway," he continued, "I been trying to make him act right, you know, settle down and shit, but he ain't trying to act right. A nigga just wanted to let you know I'm on your side with this entire situation. But, baby girl, his stubborn ass just won't listen."

Between sipping from his personal bottle, Izzi had run down a mouthful of information on his boy. Dry snitching or not, it was bittersweet to hear what Nardo was out putting in the streets about me.

For some strange reason, I couldn't make my mouth move to tell Izzi to get his hands off me. I couldn't form the words. I knew Nardo was only a few yards away, but I didn't care. Shit, he obviously didn't care who was watching him, since he was scouting for wild zoo-like creatures.

All right, Zaria, think. Move, talk, respond, do something.

I was straight tripping because Izzi's attention felt good.

Hearing him say he had my back was refreshing, especially since Nardo had obviously been talking behind it. Caught up in his stare, I realized I had never really paid true attention to how fine he was.

"I thought that was your right hand, Izzi? And why are you over here dry snitching on him? That's some underhanded, dirty shit," I finally responded to his accusations after shaking myself out of the trance.

"I wouldn't call it dry snitching, because low key, you already know, don't you? Look how he's all over that Mel chick," he tossed up in my face, pointing to the obvious. "She's ratchet as fuck, ma."

Glancing over at my daughter's father grinding, touching, and whispering with Melanie had me ready to turn the club out. This son of a bitch was cockier than ever out in public, like word wouldn't get back to me. This fool had managed to throw me off my square, flipping the script once again. Izzi was right, though; this nigga was showing me what was up. I didn't need him over here giving a commentary on it, trust.

Izzi could see the blood in my eyes and decided to add more fuel to the fire. "This ain't the first time he's dipped back for seconds with her either, Z. Your whole pregnancy—"

Before he could even finish his statement, I dropped my glass to the floor and ran off hurriedly toward the nearest exit. I had to get out of there and fast. My heart was pumping as if it was about to come out of my chest.

I moved through the crowd like lightning to the valet attendant, snatching my keys from him.

"I'll get it myself." I fought back the tears, rushing to my car.

It was still a large crowd gathered outside. Me having a tear-fest emotional breakdown wouldn't be a good look.

"Damn." I dropped my head in disbelief. "How could he banging that trick while I was pregnant? I owe him one for that." Screaming, hitting my steering wheel, I tried to gather my composure.

A phone call to my mother to see if she could keep Cidney overnight was a must. There was no way I could be up and down with her whining tonight. There was serious business in the streets to tend to with her mommy's name on it. After the infamous "you need to grow up and take care of your child" speech my mom was notorious for running down on me, I finally convinced her I would be there bright and early in the morning.

Starting the car, revving the engine, I burned rubber out of the reserved valet section, stunting hard one last time.

Doing eighty on the Lodge Freeway toward Mel's crib, I didn't know what my intentions were yet, but I knew that Operation Fuck Up Nardo's Life was in full effect. Seeing him and Mel reunited put her next on my list to feel the wrath. And I couldn't wait to square back up with Spice. As I vengefully pushed the gas pedal down, coasting in and out of traffic, I didn't notice the lights flashing behind me.

"Pull your car over. Please, pull your car over."

"What the fuck? This ain't my night," I complained, not believing my luck.

Pulling over, I adhered to all his directions, keeping my hands on the steering wheel.

For a speeding ticket, this should be in and out. I'm clean—except for this liquor on my breath.

"Good morning, ma'am. Where are you coming from or going this late?" The vanilla-face officer wasted no time interrogating me.

"I was just out getting a break from my newborn, sir. My mother has been calling, and I was just trying to make it back to her," I halfway lied, hoping he'd cut me some slack.

"Congratulations." He smiled. "Break over. Do you know why I pulled you over?"

"Thank you, sir; and, speeding." He knew, so why lie? Trying to turn on my innocent voice, I looked down to let him know I understood I was in the wrong.

"Do you have any drugs, open alcohol, or weapons on you that I should know about?"

"No." He didn't ask if I had been drinking, and I was not volunteering any info.

"License and registration."

So far, this was going as a routine stop. I ain't gonna lie; once he gave me my ticket, my plan would be back in effect. Going into my glove compartment and purse, I handed him all three items. Lucky for me, I kept my shit thorough and A-1.

"Do you know it's illegal to drive without a plate, Zaria?" Looking over the items with his flashlight, simultaneously flashing it in on me and the car, he was serious, but I was dumbfounded.

"Um, yeah."

"Okay, simple enough, huh? Then why are you out here driving illegally, without a plate and speeding?"

"What the fuck?" Caught off guard, I had to regroup fast. "My bad. I'm so sorry. I mean, what do you mean without a plate? I didn't know. Are you serious?"

Loud, hype, and knowing off rip I'd got slipped on, the officer could see this shit was totally new to me. He was laughing at my misfortune, but I didn't find that shit funny. Still, I was not in the position to tell him to pipe down.

"I'll be right back," he said, turning to walk back to his car.

I didn't really know what to expect. Besides the cops being called for me and Nardo scrapping it out from time to time—just neighbor complaints with no charges ever being filed—I'd never had a problem with the law. Before I could continue going over possible fates for me, my cell phone rang.

I recognized Nardo's ringtone. He'd picked a fine time to call. He must've heard I was around from either Izzi or some other birdie. I snatched it up off the seat quickly. Cop or not, my baby daddy was about to get the business.

"Yup, what up?" I answered angrily. "Done with that bitch?"

After a few seconds of no response, I was ready to shout louder, thinking he hadn't heard me. Then I heard a familiar voice and swallowed my words. I listened to the conversation:

"So, Nardo, what's the real word with you and Zaria? Word been ringing that y'all ain't like that no more. Keep it real with yo' girl."

"Now, why you wanna go and mention her damn name when I'm with you? My attention is all on yo' fat ass for the moment. Besides, you been on dick punishment for the last few months. That shit right there should've been lesson enough to stop gum bumpin'. You could be doing something much better with that mouth."

Hell naw! It was Melanie and Nardo's trifling asses. Now I really couldn't wait to get to this heffa's house! Looking in the rearview, I could see the cop still hard at work.

"Chill out, daddy. I'm just kickin' it with you. I'll make it up to you in a minute," she eagerly promised.

"Mel, yo' first mistake in life is ya always ear hustling, being in the next ho's business. If you minded yo' own more often and took care of your fucking self, ya wouldn't be creeping with Z's baby daddy. You'd be his."

"Hello!" I screamed repeatedly into the phone, getting no response.

I wanted Nardo to know his ass had butt-dialed me. No wonder his trifling ass hadn't checked for me. He was busy trying to get some stale pussy. And here this scummy ho had the nerve to call me so I could overhear their rendezvous. My mind was stuck. I didn't know whether I should hang up the phone or keep listening, because the cop was back at my window. Setting the phone down, part of me wanted to put it on speaker.

"Zaria, only because you have everything together, I'm going to let you go with a ticket only. Drive straight home, because if I catch you again, you're going to jail. I know you probably won't pass a sobriety test."

His warning scared me. I snatched my ticket out of his hand so fast that I had to apologize. "I'm so sorry, but thank you so much. I swear to you that I appreciate it."

"You're welcome." It seemed like it hurt for him to say the two words he'd given me a reason to say. "Take what I say seriously, and don't let me catch you on this road when I double back."

"You won't. I'm going straight home to park this car and then straight to Secretary of State first thing in the morning."

As soon as the cop got back into his squad car, I reached into the passenger's seat and clicked the button so the call would go through my speaker. They hadn't hung up. The conversation had actually heated all the way up.

"How bad do you want this pussy, Nardo?"

"Baby girl, you know that pussy got a li'l comeback. If you act right, you can always have a taste of this. Now, suck it!"

The reality of hearing Nardo's voice made my heart drop into the pit of my stomach. It felt like I was wide awake but not breathing, and then my breathing intensified. Spice had been an illusion, but Mel's quickie session was about to be engraved into my mental. Karma comes when you least expect the bitch to, and Mel being able to double back with Nardo was exactly what I'd deserved by the rules of the universe. My knowledge of how payback works didn't make me take the strike-back like a champ, however. Tears were flowing down my face, and my eyes were burning from being rubbed dry. There was no one in my car to front for, and the cop was pulling off. I'd seen and heard Nardo checking for other chicks today. The only thing left was to see him straight banging.

Finally pulling back into traffic, I merged in and went against the officer's orders, heading toward Mel's house. He'd only slowed me down. If fucking with my man was not enough, she was costing me money, too. This bitch had to pay.

I pressed down harder on the pedal as my exit, West Davison Avenue, approached. How could he still be banging that tramp? What Izzi said was true. How could he be dragging me down into the mud like that, knowing she was my enemy? He was desperately trying to tear me up and ruin me. He'd played me in the bar, and now he was about to emancipate it by doing her.

Once again, I couldn't breathe. An anxiety attack was setting in. I pushed the END button on my phone, not being able to stomach any more of what was going down on the other end. My mind was racing a thousand miles a minute. His tongue was deep inside of Melanie. His body was inside of Melanie.

My phone rang again, but I pushed IGNORE, tossing it into the back seat. Two minutes later, my voice mail alert went off. There was no telling what that message would bring to light. I was tired and frustrated. I know that God never gives you more than you can handle, but I think he must've had me confused with someone else. Hearing my phone ringing and notifications constantly going off, I turned the radio up on blast, letting the music help fuel my fire. This chick had started a war with the wrong one.

Melanie stayed on West Grand between Dexter and Wildemere, and my car automatically headed to her block. Not much had changed since me and her were friends. Her house still looked raggedy and torn the hell down, even though the inside was fairly decent last I knew.

Always having bad taste, she was the typical renter, never owning anything. Granted, the landlord obviously spent a few pennies for basic upgrades, but it definitely was not shit I'd call home. He'd done a piss-poor job on the landscaping, but I gave him an A for effort. With abandoned houses, weeds, and vacant lots tall with grass, there would be no witnesses to what I was about to do. Daringly walking up, I grabbed a brick from the yard and commenced to busting out all three of her front windows.

I hate this bitch!

Each time I heard glass shatter, my excitement grew. Jumping over the banister, I grabbed up two more bricks, rushing to the side of the house. Throwing those through what I remembered to be her dining room window, I heard even more glass breaking.

Fuck her! Trifling trick!

Letting the bricks fly in her house to knock down whatever they could, I laughed.

"Dumb ass so busy sucking a nigga dick that ain't gonna get none of these windows fixed!"

Laughing hysterically, I couldn't wait until that tramp got home and realized she'd gotten caught slipping trying to fuck me over. I causally headed back to the car, ready to do more, wishing I could burn off this steam scrapping it up with her.

"Make sure to tell that bitch Melanie that Zaria did it, and I'll be back," I announced to any neighbors or crackheads who were lucky enough to be within ear range or witnessing my wrath.

To give one old nosey lady who I saw peeking out behind her curtain even more of a show, I revved the engine again, jumping the curb onto Melanie's front lawn. Putting the car in park, I vengefully pressed down on the gas pedal, not worried about tearing up my whip. Doing five or six donuts, tearing the grass up and leaving deep tire tracks in my path, I hoped the landlord would evict her troublemaking ass.

Gunning the engine once more before throwing the car into drive, I sped off, wishing I'd done more damage. I wanted Melanie to know not to come for me! And I was more than heated she'd been so close to my car. Once home, I'd be checking for scratch marks. This was just the start of my fury-filled rage. Oh, yeah, it was feeling good!

At the first red light, I reached in my back seat for my cell phone, seeing there were two missed calls, both from Izzi.

What tip is this dude on? I pondered what he could've wanted and if I should even call him back. He could've been on some sneak-type shit or being a bug for Nardo. Ain't no telling! But I really wanted to take a chance and see what was popping. There was a sense of attraction at the club, and oddly, I was itching to find out how far it could go. If Nardo wanted to play dirty, then so be it; so the fuck would I.

CHAPTER NINE

Zaria

Of course, I couldn't resist calling Izzi back. Come to find out, he just wanted to make sure everything was all good since I left in a rush. Even though this was as wrong as two left shoes, it felt good to have him check in on me. Having time to kill, waiting on Nardo to pull back up with the skeezer who had a surprise waiting on her at home, we talked almost my entire ride back home. As he filled my ear with more bad news on ol' boy, I was topped off to the max, not knowing how to process all the newfound dirt.

"Hey, girl. I was just calling to make sure you were straight."

"Not really, but what other choice do I have?"

"More than you know, Z." I felt like he was throwing me a hint, but I was too emotionally drained to decipher it.

"Well, it sure as hell don't feel like it, but I'ma try sleeping it off. Hopefully I wake up in a better mood." I yawned. "I'm pulling up at home now."

"A'ight, cool. Are you good, or do you want me to stay on the phone with you until you get in?"

"I'm good, but thanks. I appreciate you for looking out, though." I was sincere.

"It ain't no thang, shorty."

By the time I hung up with Izzi, I'd already walked into the house and stripped down to my panties and bra.

My temples were pounding from the headache that had taken over my body. I could barely see straight. After popping a Motrin 800, I dove into my bed and crashed.

My ringtone started continuously playing, bringing me back to the harsh reality that my family would probably never be whole again. It was, of all people, Nardo. As much as I tried to fight against getting up to answer, his grips on me were still strong.

"What's good, Z?"

"So, are you still with that ho Mel or what?" I barked, smacking my lips, wiping the sleep out my eyes. I was not going to play games or just hint that I knew he was with her. "Did you get a damn room or fuck her right on the dance floor?" I cut right into him. No nonsense today; he'd know that I'd seen him. I'd had about enough crap! There was no point in the game dragging on.

"What the fuck, Z? I was not with Melanie at no club, so calm that shit down. Just when I thought I'd give yo' lunatic behind a chance to fix the problems between us, you jump stupid back on that jealous shit again."

"So, now you take me for some type of fool, Nardo? Is that it? You were with that dirtbag not too long ago and you fucked her. You're busted, so give it up." I didn't have a hint of fear or hurt in my voice. This time I wouldn't back down. I was beyond tired of his whack self always flipping the script and making me out to be the insecure, bitter woman when, in fact, he was a cheating dog.

At this point, all I heard was his heavy breathing on the phone, and that was all the extra confirmation I needed to get gangsta with his behind. "Oh, don't get quiet now since I blew you up," I demanded.

"So, you're McGruff the Crime Dog now, Z? Whoever gave you your information just wanna see you alone, and you're falling for it with yo' dumb ass." The fact that he was being oh-so-calm and not defending himself enraged me even more. If he was not guilty, he would have come through the phone. He and I both knew it.

"Fuck you, nigga. I was not trying to be a Crime Dog. I was at Floods when you two were on the dance floor dry-fucking. And while I was pulled over by the boys 'cause her ass stole my plate, my phone rang and surprise, surprise, it was Melanie's tricky, backstabbing ass and your filthy butt dragging my name through the mud." I was not holding Nardo up with my remarks. "She snitched you out by letting me hear the whole conversation. Oh, and by the way, I especially loved the part when you told her to suck your little dick! Now, think back to that."

"Z, your best bet is to lower your damn tone."

"You can go to hell with your requests, Renard. Trust when I tell you this is it. First, the bitch in the nail shop with her loose-lip ass, and now you're back to screwing Melanie? You got me acting a straight fool, looking like a big idiot in the streets."

"But—" Nardo tried to speak.

"But what, Negro?" My courage level was growing higher with every word that rolled off my tongue as I verbally attacked him. Izzi had given me extra gossip that I hadn't even hit his ass with, but it was boiling in with the rest. "Everybody in the hood is laughing behind my back because you always on the step-out, licking every stale coochie walking. And all the while, them sac-chasers only want your money and the status that comes along with dealing with you." I was really feeling myself, letting him have it full blast. "All a bitch like me ever wanted was your love and a little attention, but to hell with that pipe dream now. I'm wise to you, Nardo, and bottom line is you just ain't about shit."

I hung up on him, getting the final word, and oh boy, that shit felt good as hell. His petty lies were tiring, and I was exhausted. He called me again, and I sent him to voice mail, powering my phone off right after.

"You can miss me with all that. It's a wrap on me being your doormat," I confidently spoke out loud into an empty house, then made my way upstairs to take a long, hot shower.

I deserve so much better, was all I could think as I let the hot water soothe my pain.

If it was one good thing that came out of the night's chaos, it was that I had a date. Izzi asked if we could hang out. He promised me a good time, and I obliged. Yeah, yeah, yeah! I knew I was playing a dangerous game, but at this point, what did I really have to lose? Nardo would definitely learn his lesson if his boy was getting dibs on the cat. And if he didn't, then I was safe with my backup plan. Either way, I considered myself to be winning at this point.

Getting out of the shower, drying off, preparing to lotion up and crawl into bed, I started to get nauseated, feeling my stomach turn.

Shit, why did you mix liquor and pills? You really overdid it! What were you thinking? Knowing not to hesitate or play, I hurriedly leaned over the porcelain toilet, throwing up everything I'd eaten that day. Leaning across the toilet on my arm, I violently continued to gag and hyperventilate. *Maybe I should take this as a sign not to tread water with Izzi.*

Nardo

Who in the fuck do she think she is? I said to myself as I kept hitting the REDIAL button, calling Zaria back.

I didn't know what kinda cheap drugs she had in her system, but for sure I was going to put her smart ass back in check. She could catch me raw-dogging her moms for all I cared. All that going hard shit was not gonna be tolerated. But first I had to deal with Melanie. It was my fault for fucking with her hot fire ass. She'd set me up, and payback is a bitch.

"What up, baby?" she hummed into the phone, not knowing I had intentions of putting a hit on her head.

"Zaria told me about your little phone call, Mel, and now you got it coming," I said patiently, not wanting her to get too terrified.

"She needed to know the truth, Nardo, and hearing it from your mouth would hurt her way more than my harsh words of reality." To my amazement, she openly admitted sneak-dialing Z. Not only did Mel ramble for my phone when I ran in the gas station for some rubbers, but she'd gotten brazen enough not to even deny the allegations.

"You've played in a territory that you know nothing about, Melanie, and that's going to cost you," I warned her.

"You ain't said shit but a word, nigga. The sex is always good, but you've played both sides to the middle too much. I just wanted to hurt your baby momma's heart for stabbing me in the back, and as for you, knowing Zaria like I do, she'll handle the rest."

I didn't know what she was trying to insinuate about Z handling the rest, but I didn't have time to even question her, because I was pulling up at my baby mom's house. I hadn't planned on being there, but my car just led me in that direction. "You'll hear from me, Melanie. That shit was foul."

"Uh-huh, now I'm really shaken up, chump. Later, because thanks to your bitch, I gotta try to get my windows replaced."

Zaria

After I was finally able to get some bearings over myself, pop a few Tums, and take another shower, everything around me was starting to settle. Thinking back on Izzi's features and swag style had me feeling some sort of way. Me and him had been around each other almost daily when me and Renard first hooked up, and even though that time had been reduced to minimal run-ins when I was clowning or coming for cash, we'd never, not once, taken it past "hi and bye."

I was sorta happy that we'd agreed to hook up on some low key–type shit. While I was lying across the bed, caught up in thought, someone started indecently ringing my doorbell.

Who in the hell is at my door?

Running downstairs, almost tripping and falling over my own two feet, I was caught in mid-motion, reaching for the knob. Before I could even ask who was on the other side, my door flung open, and ain't life a bitch, Nardo was standing there, looking so pitiful with his set of my house keys clutched in his hand.

"What the hell are you doing here? Why aren't you with Mel or Spice?" I fussed, shoving him back out of the door. "When you left here earlier, you swore you were never coming back. But thanks for reminding me that you need to run that key." Standing firm with my hand out, I clutched tightly to my robe with the other. "You're cocky as hell to be showing up here after the shit you've done tonight." Shaking my head, tapping my foot, I thought, *This nigga is got me twisted. I know better, baby!*

Staring at me like a zombie, he was stuck in a daze. Maybe it was all the alcohol he'd been drinking, marijuana he'd been blowing, or the fact that I was not in the mood for being his hand puppet no longer; whatever the case, time was of the essence, and Nardo was wasting mine.

"Have you been giving my goods away, Z? My boy told me you were shaking yo' ass on the dance floor earlier, but I knew you weren't really there and he was just mistaken." His left eye twitched as he accused a bitch of everything under the sun. "Tell me he was lying, Z!"

"These ain't your goods, remember? Let you tell it, I'm played out and Spice is the next best thing, so why don't you go to her house and get the fuck out of mine?" I twisted my lips up, knowing he ain't have shit to say. "So, just be ghost. Yo' new girl and her little son, Monkey, are waiting for you. Me and Cid could outshine those dusty-looking ragamuffins on our worst day, but for some reason, you chose to lay up with that. I can't call it."

I tried slamming my door shut, but Nardo didn't budge. I shoved, pushed, and banged on his chest with my fists, but he stood tough as bricks. He forced himself all the way into the house, locking the door behind him. I stood helpless because I really didn't know what was coming next, but I didn't have to wonder long. Nardo bum-rushed me, pressed me against the wall, and stuck his tongue into my mouth. Our bodies connected, and we started kissing roughly and intensely. Even though my mind was trying to steal the emotion from my heart because I knew how filthy Nardo had gotten with other women, I couldn't fight our chemistry. It was like my body was a magnet to his.

"You're always going to be mine. This pussy is always going to be my pussy." His voice was raspy as he pressed his mouth against my ear.

"Not if you keep fucking with them other bitches." I couldn't let the moment erase the obvious.

"Fuck them. Those hoes don't have my baby." He started rubbing on my thighs and trying to part them.

Though I heard Deuce's words playing over in my mental, I couldn't resist Nardo's touch, and he knew that. Leading me to the living room, yanking me down on his lap, he started placing kisses all over my face and neck. It was on from there, because I was not about to stop him.

"Is this what you want, baby?"

"Is it what you want?" I moaned with uncertainty. My attraction for this trifling-ass nigga couldn't be denied.

Non-verbally responding, he allowed his dick to speak for itself. His hardness was pressing against me. Only having on a pair of cotton bloomers, I was not prepared for this predicament. Nardo ran his hands all over my nude body. Sliding my underwear down, I quickly stepped out of them, letting him know that we were in this together.

"Damn, let me slide in between these juicy cheeks." He spread them apart and made me moan. I was turned on. It didn't matter that just a little while ago he was banging Mel. Right here and right now, he was mine.

He lifted my small frame up by my waist, twirling me upside down. Knowing what that meant, I instinctively jumped into the sixty-nine position, sucking his dick, playing with his balls. The harder I sucked, the deeper his tongue went. He had my fuckin' head spinning, and like McDonald's, I was loving it!

Oh, shit!

My legs trembled and straight locked up at the sides of his head. He was manhandling my body in the best way. My dick-whipped ass was sprung on him bad.

After he eased himself down onto the couch without breaking our position, it was easier to give each other special attention. With my legs spread wide into a perfect V, he ate from my honey pot, taking a few dips with his fingers. The longer he licked me, the harder he face-fucked me.

My jaws were beginning to lock up and get weak. My child's father could always wear a bitch out, but he never was this damn rough with it. But, hey, I went along for the ride. Anything for baby daddy. Somewhere along the way, I convinced myself this was make-up sex.

After he bust for the first time in my mouth with me swallowing, he wasted no time throwing me onto the carpet and flipping me over. I knew that crap was gonna leave carpet burns on my knees, but fuck it!

Oh, shit! Damn! Yeah, baby! Yeah! I felt his nine and a half stiff inches rubbing up and down my crack, and I was starting to pray he didn't bang it in my asshole without any lube.

Bracing myself, I could feel my pussy juices running down my leg as my clit jumped from anticipation. Raising my left leg up to the side, he started licking my thighs while he fingered my pussy again. As soon as he found my G Spot, I wasted no time grinding and making it rain on his face.

"Oh my God, yes. I love you. Please don't leave me. Please," I moaned and begged all at the same time.

Not responding to my sex talk, he was too busy ramming his manhood deep inside me from the rear.

"Ah, you—feel—so—good." Him and his dick had me mesmerized, ready to pass out from pleasure.

"Shut up and take this dick."

Gripping both of my arms and pulling them back, he started yanking me in deeper with each stroke. This man was breaking my back in, showing no remorse. My face was getting irritated as it rubbed against the carpet.

Lord, help me!

We fucked for what seemed like hours. Nardo had the stamina of a stallion, and my pussy was sore from all the pounding. He'd had me in every position possible from the floor to the wall, then ended up busting another fat nut inside of my vagina like he didn't know what could happen.

His bad. Should've strapped up. Thinking he can keep shooting field goals and calling fouls is a bad look! Like Cidney, it won't be another abortion.

I curled up to my pillow and dozed off with a smile on my face.

I woke up at five in the morning, and Nardo was nowhere to be found. His Charger was not in my driveway any longer, and his phone was going straight to voice mail. Checking my phone, I saw that Izzi hadn't called, probably because he saw Nardo's car, so I made a mental to call and explain to him that he had just popped up unannounced. Fuck the dumb shit; I still wanted to see what tip Izzi was on. Nardo kept showing me his true intentions, so it was up to me not to keep getting played. However, this nigga deserved to feel a little burn for the simple fact of him continuously toying with my emotions.

Dragging myself out of bed with spaghetti legs from all the hardcore sexing, I pulled out a pair of jogging pants and a T shirt, sliding them both on.

"Game on. You gonna learn tonight!" I knew where he was at, and it was time to show my face, letting him know I was not playing. Grabbing my purse, with Spice's information tucked away on a piece of paper in my wallet, I typed the address into Google Maps. Snatching up a few necessary items needed for the run, I was out.

Just as I suspected, Nardo's vehicle was parked in her double car driveway next to what I assumed to be her MKX. The sun was starting to come up, so I knew to move fast. Wasting no time, I crept up, spray-painting my name in neon pink all over the passenger's side of Spice's door. Adding zigzag lines and circles definitely made me laugh. Running around the car, applying random decorations, was boosting my adrenaline. I even tagged Spice's hood by writing *CIDNEY*. To add the final touch, both of their front tires were slashed. *Fuck em!*

When I made it back to my vehicle, I started blowing the horn uncontrollably. Notoriously, I no longer cared if my presence was known, because the dirty work was done. When I saw Spice peek out the window, I waved, peeling off. Before I even made it to I-275, my phone was ringing off the hook.

"Yeah, speak, you ol' two-timing bastard!" I knew it was Nardo.

"I'm gonna kill your mothafuckin' ass, Zaria!" he hollered into the phone.

I couldn't stop laughing, and I knew that was infuriating him even more. I could hear Spice in the background, shouting in her Jamaican accent what she was going to do once she caught up with me.

"Tell her she don't want none, Nardo. Tell her that. You know how I get down, and that car is the least of her troubles." I switched my demeanor, getting serious and ready to turn my car around to whip her ass. "I'll come back and—"

"You bring your wild ass back here and I'm gonna light it up with bullets, Z," Nardo warned. "You know how I get down.

"I ain't shook! Trust that. Please, you don't scare me. I wanna see you try and pull some nonsense like that."

"I'm going to call the police on her, Nardo," I heard Spice yell, still making threats. "I'll call the law!"

"Call the po-po, ho!" I mocked, imitating Madea in Tyler Perry's *Diary of a Mad Black Woman*. Flooring the pedal, remembering my car was plateless, I merged in between two cars, coasting carefully back to the hood.

"Don't call me for a dime, Zaria. Get it how ya live for all I care, but just know when I see ya, I'm gonna beat the fuck out of you."

"Yeah, whatever. All I hear is blah, blah, blah," I screamed.

"Believe that won't be another fucking promise I break, and that's my word," he said, ending the conversation.

I started crying hysterically. I was not sad that he was really with her. Instead, my emotions were taking over because I didn't know what move to pull next. Flipping my phone over, I decided it was time to give Izzi a call. The sun had barely risen, and already this day was starting off with drama.

CHAPTER TEN

The Payback

I'd called Izzi, hollering, crying, and hyperventilating as soon as I left Spice's mini-mansion from performing. He told to meet him so he could get me straight. I had no idea how straight I was gonna feel.

I peeked from behind the thin shower curtain at him sprawled across the bed, drunk on the cum I'd left all over his ass. The last few hours were a total thrill for me, but I still couldn't believe we'd gotten a room and hooked up. He was propped up on the pillow and watching television without a care in the world, not even his home-boy. Neither of us had brought up, mentioned, or even thought about Nardo for the last few hours. We'd been too busy throwing back shots of Patrón and nibbling on edibles.

After showing my black ass for Nardo and his home-wrecker, I'd called Izzi, letting him know what all went down. He wasted no time having me detour, meeting him at the Comfort Inn on I-96 and Middlebelt. Because I was riding dirty thanks to Mel, his plan was perfect. The sun was up and dancing through the cracks of the curtains, but I wasn't ready to start my day anew. Despite Nardo's constant fronting like he could care less if I fucked the next nigga, he would piss his pants if he knew I'd given my goods up to his boy.

Fuck him. It's time to move on.

"So, bae, tell me again what went down at Spice's crib." Izzi rolled over onto his stomach.

His light-skinned complexion was so sexy to me. His long hair was braided tight like Iverson's, and his beard seemed etched into his face. Izzi kept everything crispy, just what attracts me the most. I could tell his body was choice, even with his clothes on, and the bulge I'd seen in his pants left little to the imagination. Even though I was stressed, I still was turned on by him. Stretched out with his fitted *D* hat, Detroit Cersus Everybody hoodie, and Mek denim jeans, everything about Izzi was gutter and hood but still so damn sexy.

"I left my signature on their car and flattened the tires. Some real bitter-girl-type shit," I responded. "He popped up at my house unannounced, and I gave him some. I can't even lie. When I woke up, he was gone, and that pissed me the hell off. Retaliation was a must."

Izzi fell out laughing, amused by my story. "So, yo' little ass was not scared Nardo was gonna start bustin' at you?"

"Fool, please. Nardo talks a lot of slick shit when it comes to me, but I'd like to see him lay me out." I played if off, not really sure of my words.

Thinking back on it, his threats earlier seemed colder than others. Stepping out of the shower, I stood there bold, trying to act like I had a handle on all the craziness from last night.

Tipping the bottle back again, Izzi finally looked my way then couldn't turn away. Not saying another word, he got up and walked toward me. "You wanna see me lay you out?"

My body instantly got weak. "Y–yeah," I stuttered, barely at a whisper.

Unwrapping the fluffy white towel, Izzi left me dripping wet and naked, in all of my glory. Patting me down until I was close to dried off, he led me to the king-sized bed, laying me down.

Grabbing the small courtesy bottle of lotion, he dumped almost the entire bottle into his hands before rubbing it into my body. I got lost in his touch as he massaged my shoulders, back, neck, thighs, and feet. It had been a long time since anyone had paid such close attention to my needs or wants. My eyes were getting heavy, and I felt myself drifting off to sleep.

Oh, this is so wrong, but it feels so right.

Awakening hours later to Izzi's masculine voice caused my mind to race with panic. I didn't move a muscle because I didn't want him to know that I was alert yet. My ears were open and attentive to his conversation. Damn, now my heart pumped with fear!

"She did what?" He brilliantly acted as if this was his first time hearing the tale. "Yo, man, your baby momma is straight looney for real."

I couldn't hear what the voice on the other end of the phone was saying, but I was pretty sure that I was the "looney baby momma" Izzi was referring to, and Nardo was the caller.

Please, God, let Izzi keep our secret. Please don't let it get out about us.

"I know Spice was pissed when she went down and saw the ride, right! Man, if you weren't busted before, you definitely are now. I been telling you to quit playing with these crazy bitches. Mel's gonna be next," he commented, throwing his two cents in.

Izzi was not only throwing salt into Nardo's wounds, but mine as well. I was careful to keep still. I had to. Now I knew he was talking to Nardo. I didn't dare flinch. I most positively didn't want Nardo to know I was here with his right hand. Not yet anyway.

Please, please, please, was all I could think while they continued to chop it up about business.

"A'ight, man, I'll be on the block in a few. I'm still in the waters with a hot one from last night. You know how I do," he boasted, making me remember Izzi was still a product of the dough boys who didn't wife girls.

Nardo didn't contest or hold him up much longer, now leaving me wondering what was about to pop off now.

"Hey, baby, you up? Come on and get up." Izzi nudged me, kissing the back of my neck.

Putting on my best groggy voice, even trying to sound irritated, I said, "I am now, babe. What's up?"

"Ya manz is mad hungry. Let's hit a restaurant and take care of your plate situation. Can't have you out here hot flagging bold and shit." Smiling, Izzi seemed to be much more compassionate and caring than I'd ever given him credit for. "Time for you get to up. It's three in the afternoon. You were snoring like a wild bull."

Oops, so much for that.

"Okay, I'm up. Thanks for taking me to Secretary of State, too. I was not trying to ride top streets in Livonia bold." I laughed, wishing I could've seen the look on Mel's face when she saw her house and yard.

Getting up, still keeping it secret that I'd heard his conversation, I prepared to start my first day with Izzi. We talked shit about any and everything while we got ourselves together. It felt good to have the company of a man who was so particular to my needs. We decided to keep the room for a few nights so more time together could be spent. Dang, I was really feeling him.

Unexpectedly, he was different than Nardo in so many ways. What I liked most in Izzi was how the thug in him was left on the doorstep when he came in. Nardo's mood was always tough-skin. He had seven different personalities, and all of them were fucked up.

After sharing a meal, we dipped back to the room and chilled out, watching movies before we had to part ways. The whole day was speeding past, and I had to pick up Cidney from my mom's. And of course, Izzi had business in the hood to deal with. It was agreed that whatever happened in the room stayed in the room because we weren't ready to face the world with our secret friendship. Hell, I was feeling Izzi something terrible.

On my way from the Comfort Inn, I stopped by my girl Kimmie's to keep her posted on what had went down. And no doubt, I wanted to tell her to keep her ear to the hood so I could know Nardo's every move.

"Ohhh, hey, Z-gurl." Kimmie got loud. "What's up wit' you?" She greeted me as I walked into the crowded nail shop. The spot was undeniably going to make money today while trying to make these hood hoes look a little bit better.

"Kimmie, if you only knew what I've been through since I left here. You know Nardo had the nerve to claim old girl that I beat down the other day," I said, putting my hand to my chest, imitating sheer shock.

"Oh, no. Shut yo' head, black girl. You lie to Kimmie. You lie." She dramatically waved her ever-present nail file. Damn, her Korean accent was so funny to me. She always had to mix it up with her best black homegirl voice.

"Yeah, since then he's abandoned me and Cidney to be with that tramp. Can you believe that?"

"Me not believe that bullshit, home gurl. You know niggas ain't shit. He come back home. You see. You two be on that back-forth shit all the time. Nardo change tune and come back," Kimmie promised like she knew for sure and had a special fortune cookie that was backing her words up. "I see him at club other night. Him big fool."

I had to give Kimmie a pass this time to dog Nardo out, because she was right. He was being a fool if he thought that whore was a substitute for me.

"Yeah, I know. Hey, has Melanie been in here lately?" I probed, trying to find out if she'd heard anything about me busting out her windows.

"Oh, no. Her nails must look raggedy. She ain't been in my shop for seven to eight weeks now. Probably need fill-in bad, unless all the acrylic has grown off them ugly fingers of hers." She started looking strange as she bobbed her head. "Why you ask? You see her at club too? Dancing?"

"Yeah, Kimmie, stop frontin'. I saw her and Renard at the bar, and she was all on his dick." I checked her quick, fast, and in a hurry. "You know me. I had to go tear something out the wall after peeping that mess."

"Awww, Z gurl, stop let Nardo get you to do stupid silly shit. You fuck round and pay big, big price for that."

"I ain't even worried, Kimmie."

I finished putting her up on all the miscellaneous drama that had occurred since I'd last seen her. But intentionally, I left out the part about Izzi. That was a top notch secret. "Keep your ear to the streets," I demanded, walking out the door as my cell began to ring.

"You not worry. Kimmie call you, Z gurl." She waved her hand, still bobbing her head. "Kimmie call youuuu."

My cell kept ringing. My mother was calling. I had to pick up Cidney. After all I'd been going through, I was neglecting my baby girl, who didn't deserve to be set out in the wind to dry.

Picking her up from my mom's house was more argument than I intended. After she got on my head about leaving my one and only child on her while I was chasing behind some street punk, as she always called Nardo, and going down her long, drawn-out list of her rules

I'd broken, I was finally able to get back home. I laid Cid down for a nap and cleaned the house from top to bottom. When she woke up, I gave her a long bath and greased her skin. Even though she was only a few months old, I always kept her in cute clothes and dolled up. I read her a few books and played with her rattles and other loud, annoying toys with her. She was just into the stage of smiling when you did something goofy, and she was melting my heart. I held Cidney closely and sang lullabies to her until she fell back to sleep. It was good to feel as if I was connecting to my daughter. She deserved a good mother.

I then opted to call my gynecologist, setting up an appointment. It was time for my checkup, and plus, the need for birth control was critical. Seeing that Nardo was not going to be in my life meant that there was a strong possibility that I'd have multiple sexual partners.

The rest of the evening was not as eventful as the previous days. I just chilled around the house, trying to come up with my next moves. I didn't even have my cell phone turned on because I didn't feel like anyone calling me with some he-say/she-say garbage to set me off. It was good to not have the world on my shoulders for once. I was supposed to meet up with Izzi at the room, but I didn't know what time, so fuck it. I was going to catch up on some much-needed rest.

Nardo

"You a straight punk nigga for even letting Zaria come and fuck your shit up like that," Izzi affirmed, fearlessly walking around my car, taking a good look at my baby momma's work.

"Izzi, believe me, man. That's been the only thing on my mind is how she wild out." I shook my head. "Spice is ready to damn near call up the Jamaican Mafia and run up in Z's house, but I already confirmed that was a definite no go."

"What you mean, a no go? If a bitch spray-painted my ride, I would run up in her house first, with my people behind me for reinforcement," Izzi instigated, jumping shotgun to head to our Connect, E.

Izzi had been talking way out of pocket about Zaria, and I was not feeling that at all. Not wanting to beef out with my manz over a female was a must, especially since Zaria had damaged my ride.

Spice was still on the nut about that night, and quiet as it was kept, I couldn't even blame her. She hit my pockets like crazy this morning, even making me commit to going on a trip with her and little man. I had been sucked into being stepdaddy to her son, and the funny part about it was it didn't even bother me.

I wanted a good relationship with Cidney, but her moms made that damn near impossible. Spice's point of view was to leave the situation alone, because she didn't want to deal with my baby momma on any level, and no doubt, all things considered, I could feel her. Yet, a part of me still loved Zaria, and it was not questionable if she was the best in bed. Hands down, or should I say ass up, she was good with it. But her evil ways and attitude were unappealing. The few good qualities buried deep weren't worth the headache she brought to the table.

Zaria was my past, and Spice was my future. I had a new family—just like that.

CHAPTER ELEVEN

Zaria

Life had been chaotic and stressful for me over the last few months. With all the drama I'd been dealing with and starting behind Nardo's bullshit, my body had become drained and exhausted. I was naked in my bed, cuddled up to my pillow, and sleeping sound as hell. I'm talking about snoring-and-having-drool-falling-from-my-mouth sound asleep. That was, until my eyes popped open to some bullshit.

I laid there still and sound for a few seconds, thinking that the intrusion was a dream, but it was not. My reality was grim. The female's voice got louder, and her knocks turned into pounds. I threw the covers off my body and woke all the way up. Ol' girl, whoever she was, was about to catch a beatdown. I don't like getting lied to, cheated on, or stirred up out of my sleep.

"Bring ya filthy-cunt-having ass outside and catch this fade, Zaria," the girl shouted then started pounding up and down my door even harder.

Grabbing my phone and my pistol from my nightstand, I was moving so fast to put on a pair of panties that I stumbled over my feet and almost fell to the floor.

"Don't make me come through this muthafucka, because I will." She called herself threatening me, but I was about to hit her with the ultimate surprise.

As soon as my foot hit the first step to come down the staircase, I loaded a bullet into the chamber of my nine. I was itching to send a hot one through the door, watch her body fall through the peephole, and then carry my tired ass back to bed.

"Nine-one-one, what's your emergency?" the operator answered my call.

I cringed at the sound of her voice. I hated that I was about to converse with the cops, but I had to play the responsible role as a parent and protect Cidney. If the worst happened, I needed my ass to be covered.

"Do you, but make it at your own risk. If you come through that door, though, you will catch what I have for intruders." I used key words I knew the 911 operator would hone in on, then gave her my address.

"And what is that? Some free pussy?" I caught onto ol' girl's voice and dropped my phone, wishing I hadn't called the police in the first place. It was Melanie.

I already knew Melanie was probably on my porch with revenge on her mind behind me busting out a few of her windows, but I didn't give a fuck about her reasons, and I was not about to give her a pass. It was gonna be an eye for an eye with us until one of us died, as far as I was concerned. Snatching the door open, I damn near yanked my own knob out of the socket.

"You'd suck on my pussy too if I got down like that, ho. Play with it." I said some shit that I knew would get underneath her skin, then waved my pistol in the air. "Now, why in the fuck are you on my porch?" She seriously didn't want it with me.

"Girl, bye. Are you supposed to be some type of a threat to me now? A bully? You better guess again," she bossed up, adding fuel to the already scalding situation. "Your ass better give me the money for this fucking eviction notice 'cause of those windows, or it's about to be on!"

She was waving paperwork around that was unfamiliar to me, never having a Thirty-sixth District landlord/tenant issue.

This chickenhead didn't know I was about my business since I'd dropped my load. Things were real now, and that ho was fake and lightweight to me. The fact that she was on my doorstep had me fuming even more. "Mel, you're one lonely, jealous bitch, and that's so pathetic," I said, moving closer in her direction. "That's why you had to call me the other night, letting me know you were getting some of that dry dick. I pity you! You wanna be me so bad, but you can't. You just can't, so stop playing yourself!"

Momentary silence filled the front porch.

"Me, lonely? Please get your facts straight, you gutter rat tramp. Nardo only wanted yo' ass for some hard back, but you fucked around and trapped him with Cidney. So, don't get all celebrity. He's still just on yo' team for the baby, but trust, bitch, you been fouled out a long time ago," Melanie finally rebutted.

"Oh, yeah, ho. I'll put my hands on you and we'll see who gets fouled out first. Game time. Now what? I know you didn't come over here for idle chit-chat."

Her nappy, four-month-old weave was about to get snatched out. What Mel said about me being fouled out after Cidney's birth cut like a knife because I secretly knew it was true, just like Kimmie's words from the other day, but I had to keep my front up. That was another one of my mother's famous rules: Never, ever show a chick what hand I was holding.

"Come on now, Z. In your dreams you couldn't bang bows with me, so don't get ignorant. We both know if you didn't have that gun—"

"If I didn't have this gun what?" I challenged, leaning backward, placing my burner on the table in the entrance.

"Then I'd tap that ass."

"Run up, ho. Please run the fuck up," I begged, wishing that she would. "I don't have any more words for you, just these hands, and you're still just flapping your lips. Quit prolonging this ass-whooping."

Melanie did a surprise move by pulling out a box cutter, rushing up on me, quick like lightning. "I see you not talking your run-up shit now, are you?" she taunted as she knocked me up against one of my concrete pillars. Her voice sounded like a madwoman.

I didn't expect her to have a blade or even yoke me up like that. *Why'd I put my fucking gun down?* I'd underestimated Melanie.

It was then I realized she was just as bitter and scorned as I was because Nardo had left her too—but for me. I was her Spice. He'd played a game with her heart and was still playing it. In her mind, I was her life's fuck-up, because since him officially dumping her, Mel's status level around the way had dropped drastically. No more VIP, no more Las Vegas trips, no more car notes getting paid, and no more spur of the moment shopping sprees: the same terrible, depressing fate that probably awaited me if I didn't play my cards right.

But I couldn't let her know that I now knew how she felt, that I sympathized with her anger. *Fuck her!* She was still beneath me, so to hell with her feelings. Ms. Thang had some nerve stepping to where me and my child laid our heads and then pulling a blade! When I got a chance, she would soon have to pay, right or wrong, reason or not.

I know I took Nardo from her, so technically I was wrong as two left shoes. And I also knew I was the one who started it, going to her house first, but so fucking what? This stank whore lived directly in the center of the hood! Her rowdy, forty-ounce-taking-it-to-the-head, unemployed neighbors were used to that type of bullshit jumping off. Everybody on my quiet block had jobs—nine-to-five, salary-paying jobs at that. They weren't the type of neighbors that would hesitate to call the law. They would have the cops at your front door for having the volume turned up too loud while 50 Cent's drama *Power* was on.

Melanie seemed overly amused as I felt her hot, tainted breath whisper in my ear. "Cidney ain't did shit but make his ass run for the border, dumb ho! And now that child ain't gonna have a mother to look up to. Your decisions done fucked you up."

I wanted Melanie's head badly, but any move I made could be fatal to me, so I kept still and bit down on my bottom lip as if that gave me strength.

"I mean, what did you think, Zaria? Did you honestly think you were going to come and pull that ignorant stunt at my house with no consequences? Be for real. Everything costs," she said tightening her squeeze.

I began to feel the pressure of the tip of the box cutter against my neck.

"Drop the weapon!" I suddenly heard a police officer yell. "Drop your weapon right now."

I closed my eyes, thanking God personally for saving my life. Melanie's soul was hurt, and she was ready to take me out of the game. How could this happen? I was on the verge of paying the ultimate price for loving Nardo, who was no more than a two-timing, backstabbing, cheating dog.

"It ain't over, Zaria," she swore, dropping the box cutter to the ground and raising her hands in the air. "It ain't."

The police hurriedly cuffed her before shoving her to the car while reading her rights. I couldn't believe Melanie was ready to go as far as to kill. I informed the officer that I'd be at the station to press charges first thing in the morning. After making sure I was okay and everything around the perimeter of the house looked safe, they drove off. I stared dumbly as a deranged-faced Melanie mouthed the words "I'm gonna kill you" from the back of the car.

Whenever she got out, we were definitely going to have to settle the score, because the road we were headed on definitely promised fatality. At this point, I was unsure who would end up in a body bag.

Ashamed in front of my neighbors, I dropped my head, walked back inside the confines and security of my house, and called Nardo. He shot me straight to the voice mail, so I left a message.

"Melanie was just over here, and now she's on her way to jail. Please control your tramps, little boy. One," I said, hanging up and then calling Izzi.

There was no answer for him either, but I was not about to leave him a message. That was just evidence for a person to find out we were kicking it. I would call back private in a few. Me and Izzi were definitely about to be getting it in.

In the meantime, I got Cidney together to drop off at the babysitter. I felt like a bad mom, always dropping her off and not bonding during these critical months where she was supposed to be forming an attachment with me, but my mental was too fucked up behind Nardo to even fully love myself. I did not want to be one of those mothers who took all of life's frustrations out on her child. I did not want Cidney growing up to resent me, or have a burden on her back about her father that was not hers to carry.

At the end of the day, I didn't want to holler at Cidney for simply being a baby, and I wanted her to form her own opinion and relationship with Nardo. In spite of what cruel shit he might spit at me about me trying to trap him with her, or that she could belong to any random nigga in the hood, I knew that those words were only to hurt me and would never get repeated to Cidney. He knew good and damn well that little girl was a spitting image of him.

After I got Cidney's diaper bag packed with enough diapers, onesies, clothes, and toys, I pre-made a few bottles with four ounces of formula each. That was the least I could do to help the babysitter out since I wouldn't be there to help her soothe my newborn once she cried out, hungry. Being honest, I had not cuddled and fed Cidney in so long that I might not even know how to appease my li'l one. I had to hurry up and take care of this Nardo situation so I could get my mental right and start being a better mother.

Deciding to keep it simple, especially because I didn't know if one of Nardo's jump-offs would try to catch me slipping again, I tore up my dresser drawers looking for something to wear that was cute yet comfortable enough to kick some ass in. After this morning, I was not only ready for, but I was down for whatever.

I ended up throwing on a pair of tight-fitting stonewash jeans, a plain T-shirt that was a size too small on purpose so it would make it seem like I had more chest than I actually have, and a fresh pair of Air Max. I loved wearing running shoes because they're geared for working out and strengthening leg muscles, so they automatically enhanced my glutes. My booty cheeks were banging when I wore tight jeans and leggings. I could not wait to finish getting my body right so I could stunt hard on the city again.

Izzi

Zaria was without a doubt the most real woman I'd been around in a while. Her heart was just torn, making it hard to break through her tough exterior. I was not going to stop trying, though. I did not care that she had Nardo's daughter. I didn't care that she had a short fuse to her ticking time bomb. In my book, she just required a little effort and a whole lot of attention to mend the broken heart that Nardo was responsible for. I had watched my homeboy run through plenty of females while he had been holding Zaria hostage, but it wasn't my place to step on his toes or speak to her the truth. That was, until I started feeling some type of way about shorty. I'd fucked mad females from around the way whose only mission in life was to chase paper day in and day out. What attracted me to Z was her loyalty and constant chase to have her family.

Now, don't get me wrong; I ain't no fool. Zaria loved money, of course, but with Nardo, she held my peoples down. I envied that dude because he had a girl, I mean a woman, who genuinely cared. Low key, no matter how hard I tried fighting the shit, I was immediately attracted to Zaria from jump. When I first laid eyes on her, I lusted after her body and her gorgeous smile. I knew, given enough time, Nardo would mess the relationship up, like all his previous ones, because he had no control with his females. He gave them the world financially but was totally unaware of the fact that a woman needed more than that from a man.

It was only a matter of time, and now I was going to step directly on his toes to get her. You could say I was playing the devil's advocate role. It's cool; I was. I'd been stunting to Nardo off rip that Z was no good, and being that dude can never think for himself, he fell for that shit and swung all the way with Spice. Ol' girl was foul, and it was no doubt in my mind. Now, trust when I say this, and I'm not hatin; he'd learn not to deal with certain sac chasers. That island rat was gonna teach Nardo a real lesson.

I watched as Zaria got out of the car in the hotel parking lot. Damn, she looked good! Her hair fell with curls, and the bangin' curves of her body looked mad sexy. Looking up to the window, Z caught me staring. She smiled and waved. Damn, Nardo was dumb.

"Hey, Izzi." She grinned, finally coming into the room and hugging me before getting comfortable. "What's up?"

On cue, I ran my hands all over her back, even caressing her soft booty. My mind was thinking of all the kinky positions I could twist her body up in. The sex with Zaria was always dynamite. She felt so good in my arms that I'd gotten an instant rise.

"Hey, girl. I missed you fa sho'," I whispered in her ear, tugging on it with my lips.

"I see." Zaria couldn't resist tugging at the bulge in my pants.

We sat down on the couch, and she kicked off her shoes. Her perfectly pedicured feet went up into my lap, massaging my nuts. She then told me her version of what went down with Melanie's murder attempt on her. Zaria's existence was full of drama, and all because of Nardo. Secretly, I schemed and would find a way to make homeboy pay for hurting her. I just honestly couldn't believe she'd taken so much abuse and still was going on. All I wanted to do was be a real nigga for her.

That night, I'd taken every piece of Zaria. I made love to my newfound goddess in the most exotic positions, pleasing her in every way possible. With every deep stroke, I was trying to sex the problems out of her. After it was all said and done and she lay fast asleep in my arms, I made the final decision. I was going to take Nardo out of the game so it could be just me and her. It was the only way. A gangster like me had fallen in love.

CHAPTER TWELVE

Nardo

Me and Izzi made contact with E, the connect, and grabbed some major weight. We had it all mapped out, and in our minds, this lick was about to make us kingpins. We had been plotting, planning, and putting both of our hard heads together for months before making this move so we could come up with an airtight hustle that could keep us both paid. Me and my homie didn't want to come up and fall off within the same lifetime, but stay on and put a crew of li'l fellas on to work beneath us.

I was planning on spreading weight through the west side of Detroit, while Izzi was plotting on making the east side his personal playground. The potency of our product was going to speak for itself and end up shutting crews down. In our minds, the takeover was going to be easy.

In addition to running dope through the streets, Izzi and I wanted to start making moves that other pushers hadn't thought of. We were about to be on some top secret, government official-type shit. And that's kinda where the idea came from. This cat that bought coke from me gave me a lump sum out of his first of the month check, and I gave him a line of credit in return. Once that lump sum was done, he was either cut off until the first rolled around again, or I'd give him the credit for his word that he would pay when his check came. Him using his Social Security check as collateral made him loyal, which would happen once I started extending this option to a few of the buddies he got high with.

We were going to put together a crew to serve out of an inpatient treatment home, and we already had connects on the inside. I couldn't make a living off a fiend being clean, so I was not pushing for that recovery bullshit. The day me and Izzi walked up in there with fresh sneakers on our feet, Cartier glasses on our faces, and threw some cash on the table, the medical assistants went crazy over who was going to fuck with us and become our li'l crony. Those hot and ready hoes were willing to do a lot more than let us through the front door with some baggies, though. One of the shorties had been blowing up my phone day in and day out ever since.

I pulled up at the mall to see what Elite Jewelers had to offer. I was going to get Spice something that was real nice since she'd taken a savage-like ass-whipping and her car got vandalized. I'd already gotten her a fresh paint job, but she needed a little more reassurance that I was 100 percent in her corner.

My phone kept ringing from a private caller, and I didn't do private calls, so I kept shooting it to my voice mail. Zaria had left a message when she called from her number earlier, but I deleted it quickly. For all I knew now, it was her salty ass calling back to start her extra shit for the day.

"Hey, baby, where are you at?" Spice asked when I called her to check in. I didn't know what had gotten into me, but she was getting me open.

"Taking care of business. Why don't you get little man together so we can go out and eat tonight?"

"Now, that's what's up, babe. Can you make sure your baby momma won't be playing Sir Stalk-a-lot tonight?" she questioned sarcastically. "Because somebody has been playing on my phone."

I sighed, tired of the drama. "I got it, and I will take care of her. Don't even worry about it." I tried putting her mind at ease. "All I want you to do right now is get ready because I will be pulling up within the hour. Cool?" I wanted to make sure she heard me and understood what I wanted her to do.

"Yeah, cool. I will make sure I'm ready." Spice fell in line.

"Good. I'll see you then." I ended the call with her then clicked over to the private incoming call. It was clear they were resilient and wouldn't stop calling, and I decided to answer to make sure it wasn't an issue with Cidney. "Speak your peace and speak it quickly before I hang up," I spat with annoyance, letting them know as soon as I answered that I was pissed behind them continuously calling when it was clear I was purposely sending them to my voice mail.

"Nardo, your stank-ass baby momma had me locked up earlier, and I need a thousand to make bail. I'm at the Northeastern District. Please tell me that you've got me." Melanie's voice sounded off.

"And what you calling me for? Whatever stupid shit yo' ass did is on you. Besides, last time we spoke, you was like fuck me anyway. All I've got for you is a li'l advice. Get friendly with one of those buddies you're bunking with to see if they'll teach you how to make a shank so you can protect yourself. I'm out. One." I was making fun of Melanie's circumstances as I chuckled loudly then hung up in her face.

Mel must have had a psychotic meltdown and gotten some super strong drugs when she got locked up to think I was about to run to her rescue. Not only would my savage ass not be caught down at a police department willingly, but I wouldn't cash out on Melanie anyway. She wasn't my girl. I only hit her off with a good stroke from time to time. The only thing I owed Melanie was a crippling orgasm.

Melanie's random phone call, however, did do something for me. It put me back on my square and up on game to watch my back for the moves my baby momma was making. She'd gotten Melanie locked up and had not called repeatedly, texted, or sent a brick through my window with a note tied to it to tell me. Something was wrong with that. Normally she was all about getting my attention.

I sat back and started thinking long and hard about Zaria's track history of craziness. First, she'd stomped down on Spice in the nail shop, coming home to me in a premeditated rage. Then she wrecked our cars right in Spice's driveway on a solo mission I was still shocked she'd pulled off. And now she was moving silently, which meant I really needed to be worried because she now knew I was taking care of Spice's son. There was no doubt in my mind that she was brokenhearted and on a vengeance spree.

Melanie called a few more times, but I didn't waste my time answering. It was not a thing she could do for me on the inside. Besides that, I had a life to live and a li'l family to keep content.

I knew the mall was going to be crazy crowded before walking through the entrance because I almost witnessed two fights in the parking lot over spots. Not wanting my car dinged up, I preferred parking in the back, so I swooped into an empty spot with no problem and kept focused on why I was at the mall in the first place. I like staying clean and jumping fresh, but like many men, I hated the mall. I usually shopped in the early morning hours when there wasn't a crowd, and today was a reminder why.

Every store I went in was jumping with customers. They were either shopping, in line to purchase, or popping off with the workers who already had stank attitudes because they were underpaid and highly disrespected. I ended up walking out of three female clothing stores, not being able to tolerate the foolery that was going down within them. I loved pretty faces, banging bodies, and quiet mouths. I had enough drama and nonsense coming from Zaria.

Finally finding a jewelry store that wasn't overcrowded, probably because it was not income tax season, I went in my pocket and cashed out on a tennis bracelet for Spice that I knew she'd adore. On the low, she had been pawning pieces that her father sent before he dismantled their father/daughter relationship, so I knew she would appreciate me adding value back to her stock. The gift wouldn't come without strings, though. She was gonna have to fall back on that "go to the pawn shop" shit and let me hold her down like a real man is supposed to do. If the wrong person saw her, the embarrassment in the streets I'd feel would never be lived down.

Since I had a few extra dollars in my pocket that I could play around with, I ended up buying Spice a ring I was going to present to her as thanks for being loyal to me in the face of Zaria being a threat to her. I was not proposing or promising anything but to protect her if Zaria came back to battle with her again. My delivery would be so clear, precise, and worded perfectly that she wouldn't have any other choice but to accept the truth that her position would remain as my live-in main chick. I'd let her use the title "boyfriend," though.

The man in me could not walk out of the mall without making sure both of the kids I was labeled as the provider for were taken care of. And by right, I started with Cidney. Regardless of me and Zaria's relationship, my li'l one wouldn't be out here on the streets getting strolled around without name brand clothes on her tiny body and cute, girly kicks on her feet. I would be dropping the bags off on either Zaria's porch or her mother's house to keep our contact to a minimum so I wouldn't have to go in her grill. Zaria and I could be cordial, but only after we'd had some time to cool down.

Not sure of Cidney's size, I picked out an attractive salesgirl and showed her a picture that I had taken when I was at Zaria'a house the other day. I wanted to watch her booty cheeks bounce and her breasts jiggle in the low-cut shirt she had on while I was shopping for my daughter. After she finished complimenting me on having an adorable twin, she picked out a gang of outfits and matching shoes. I got shorty's number after she hooked me up with her discount. I knew it would be beneficial for my pockets to plug up the plug since I'd be cashing out on girl clothes for years to come.

Before leaving the mall, I copped me a fresh pair of kicks and threw a pair of matching ones on the bill for Spice's son, too. I had an addiction to shoes and was gonna have li'l homie strung out on 'em too if I stayed around playing like his daddy. My sneaker collection was sick. Whenever I bought a style of shoes, I bought two pair, so I could put one pair up and floss the other. Well, let me correct that. I bought three pair so her son could floss like me when we went out. He was not mine, but it wasn't no thang to be fresh like me. Besides, he was as close to a son as I was going to have for a very long time. I had to do for Cidney; I could do for Spice's son if I wanted to, or not. I liked having that freedom.

Once I got back in the car, I ignored the person waiting for my spot and rolled up a fat one to drive home to. Busting a fat nut was always better when I was high, and

I knew Spice was about to come up off some neck once I surprised her with these gifts.

"Honey, is that you?" Spice called out when she heard the door open.

"Yeah," I answered, stepping over the threshold to the aroma of jerk chicken.

Spice could cook like a Caribbean chef, and she did it all the time. Unlike Zaria, she did not complain or keep it simple or the same. There was always a plate of food for me in the microwave when I got home from hustling or cheating.

"Hey," Spice sang, meeting me in the hallway. "I'm ready just like you said to be."

"Good girl." I bent down and kissed her lips, then handed her the jewelry store bag.

I waited on her to open it and thank me with a million kisses and a great big hug. Then I told her she better not be down at the pawn shop again unless she was ready to end what we had going on.

"You have my word on it." She made a promise that she vowed to keep.

I then took the ring from the bag and gave her my planned-out speech. I'd fine-tuned and critiqued it in the car on the way home and delivered it perfectly. I was not sure if she heard any words, though, 'cause she was too busy unbuckling my pants to get my penis down her throat.

After her stomach was loaded up and my balls were unloaded, we happily loaded up in the truck with her son buckled in the back seat. With my day going good, I should have never planned on making a stop in the hood, especially as a family, like the one that Zaria was dying to have with me.

"Baby, as soon as I pick up my money off the block to sponsor our day out, I'm going to turn my phone off and let Izzi handle business. Are you good with that?" I didn't care about her answer, but hey, I could put up a front like I cared.

"Yup, honey. I'm good." She was staring at her ring in a daze, probably thinking about exactly what I told her not to.

Zaria

Izzi and I had a spectacular, unbelievable night. I truly felt like there was a deep connection made between us, but I didn't know for sure, and I was not about to jump to any conclusion and get my feelings hurt. There'd been enough of that going on.

Though I was sleeping with Izzi, I still had to think smart and question what his motive really was. Was he trying to score with Nardo's baby momma just for ego's sake? Was I supposed to be a distraction for his bigger plan? Did he really like me like I thought I liked him? Or hell, was I just caught up in the attention he was giving me, and not really in him? I could not let me being lonely and desperate for Nardo's loyalty for all of these years fade to dark now that I was fuckin' his best friend.

Regardless of how many different ways I answered the questions or tried playing out many different scenarios he could have been using me for, I decided to let go of my concerns and enjoy hooking up with him. I deserved a li'l fun, a lot of attention, and some good-ass stroke on a consistent basis. I was down to ride for however long whatever we had going lasted, and it did not have to have a label to keep a life.

Izzi was a distraction from Nardo. When I was with him, I felt so much power and control of my feelings. Izzi was like the medicine for my heartbreak. You know what they say about having another man to get over the ex-man. When I was laid up with Izzi, I was not crying and throwing a pity party for myself. There were not any tears, but me screaming, "Fuck Nardo, his bitches, his lies, and all the drama that came along with him!"

The only part of the date that went berserk and that I still couldn't wrap my mind around was that I let Izzi raw without a condom. Although the skin-to-skin strokes felt so much better and made the multiple orgasms much more intense, I knew that slip-up was something that couldn't happen again—let alone continuously happen. It was one thing to get over Nardo with Izzi, or even enjoy the dick so much that I thought a relationship could come from it, but I would walk the plank straight into hell before having two babies by best friends. All things happen for a reason, and I was thankful for my doctor's appointment I was about to be early for.

Checking in with Cidney's babysitter to make sure all was well, I was on my merry way to get an exam and the much-needed birth control I was not leaving her office without. I was hoping to get the shot for instant protection so I would not miss a beat in getting some more skin-to-skin strokes from Izzi. As nasty as it sounds, I thought about him while spreading my legs on the stirrups, which made me wetter during the exam.

I went to the doctor happy because I was going for birth control, but I ended up leaving the office in complete denial and ready to see a psychiatrist for depression.

"No, no, no!" I cried out, slamming my fist onto the steering wheel, drawing attention to myself.

My legs were weak, and my body trembled. Life was nothing but a huge, twisted spiral that only seemed to go in a downward direction for me. I know they say knowledge costs and that karma is a bitch, but I couldn't keep taking the mighty blows.

Feeling remorse, I dialed Nardo's number. I was not expecting him to answer, but I was still let down when his voice mail popped on. There could have been an emergency with Cidney and he would not have known, busy ignoring me to prove a point that I was not important. I carefully chose my words when I left him a voice mail, not wanting to set him off and give him another reason to hate me. I then proceeded to follow through with a text message that I was not on no bullshit but really needed to speak with him about something urgently important.

I sat in the parking lot of the clinic for ten minutes, clutching the positive pregnancy test results, waiting on Nardo to call back. The only reason I pulled out of my spot was because the security guard asked me to move for another patient.

My heart was torn in a million pieces, and I was more than confused. On my drive to the doctor, my mind was racing about how Izzi might have felt about me; leaving from the doctor I had new sets of much more serious questions. Like, should I keep this unborn, innocent baby, or should I give it back to God?

My mental state was confused, and going through an emotional pregnancy at this stage in the game would only deteriorate the situation. I was trying desperately to hold on to my sanity. Me and Nardo were beyond the point of reconciliation. Unsure if I was even capable of living my own life for nine months, I grieved. Could I really carry and produce another one of his seeds? I knew there wasn't a chance for it to be Izzi's baby because the time didn't add up.

My phone barely rang one time before I answered it in a fatigued murmur. "Hey, what's up," I whined to Nardo. "I'm glad you called me back."

"What's the damn emergency, Z? Is Cid okay?" He wasted no time with formalities or putting on a front like he was concerned or cared about me.

"Yeah, she's good, but we have to talk."

There was a silence on the phone that made me think he'd hung up on me. Right when I was getting ready to pull the phone from my cheek to check, he cut into me with short patience.

"Well, be quick about whatever it is you've gotta say. Just be mindful that I'm not in the mood for your bullshit."

Quick to bite my tongue so I would not snap on him and get hung up on before I was able to get out what I needed to say, I stuck to the game plan of playing it cool.

"I would rather talk to you about it in person." My voice cracked from me holding back the tears.

Although I usually tried to play tough and like I could stomach all the gut-wrenching blows Nardo delivered, right at this very second, I wanted him to hear in my voice that something was terribly wrong with me on the inside. I wanted him to hear that I was emotional on a whole different level.

"I ain't even trying to see you, Z." He harshly rejected my plea without hesitating.

"But—" I went to beg for him to hear me out but was cut off.

"But nothing, Zaria. I tried playing cordial and cool with you the other day, but you came up out of your bag with some bullshit, like you always do. It is draining dealing with you, and unfortunately, today is not the day. So, if nothing is wrong with Cidney, don't call this phone back after I hang up on you. As tough as you've been acting lately, you shouldn't be crying any damn way."

"Oh my God, Nardo. Stop going off and please listen," I begged, starting to panic because I did not want him to hang up.

I knew from arguing with Nardo over the years and countless times that he would hang up on me and ignore a hundred and one calls of mine effortlessly. He was not one of those dudes who would keep answering to hang up, or even turn his phone off so I'd eventually stop calling or fill his voice mail up. Nardo would mock and antagonize me, in an attempt to break me down and hurt me worse, by letting the phone ring over and over again, just to keep me thinking I had a chance of him answering. Instead of fighting against him leaving, I should be running the other way. But I wasn't. I was actually more locked in with Nardo than I actually planned this time around.

"Bye, Z—" Nardo got ready to say my name and hang up, but I cut him off.

"I'm pregnant, and it is yours."

There was an uncomfortable silence on the phone that scared me—right before Nardo cursed me out. "Quit calling me for attention with yo' lying ass. There's no reason to think that news is for me. Call yo' other nigga," he responded like I was a joke then hung up.

I tried calling back, but his line was going directly to voice mail. That made my blood boil because that was not how he usually rolled.

"For real, Nardo? That's how you wanna play me?" I growled, mad as hell that I could not get through. I would rather call and get ignored than be immediately shut down. My heart sank each time I was shut down.

Swerving my car over to the curb, I gritted my teeth, hearing my rims scratch against the concrete. I was really tripping and about to tear my shit up unnecessarily, which meant I really needed to take a pause for the cause and breathe. Nardo was usually the one who took my car in for oil changes, repairs, and to even get air in the tires. With us beefing, I would be stranded for sure if something came up wrong with it.

After inhaling and exhaling a few times with my eyes closed, my heart rate did not slow down. I popped my eyes open and said "Fuck!" trying to get a grip. I did not have any of my godbrother's green goodness to help ease my pain, and I was fed up with Nardo always pushing my back against the wall. I was about to start doing some shoving of my own.

Dumping the contents of my purse out onto the front seat, I fumbled through all the junk in search of the ripped sheet of notebook paper with Spice's number on it. Almost starting to panic that I had mistakenly thrown it away, I came across it and held it up to sky like it was a hundred-dollar bill. To me, her seven digits were like money. I dialed them with a smile on my face, making sure to press the notorious *67 to make my identity show up as anonymous.

Had it been me seeing an unknown call coming through on my cell phone screen, I would have sent it to my voice mail for screening purposes. Spice's dumb ass answered, though, in her creepy Jamaican accent that made my skin crawl, and after only three rings. My smile faded as soon as I heard how chipper she was—with my baby daddy and a few other familiar voices in the background.

"Hello? Can you hear me? Hello," Spice kept trying to get me to respond, though she did not know it was me.

A small part of me felt like Spice did know it was me, however, and that she was rubbing her position in my face. I now know firsthand how Melanie must have felt the day I intentionally answered Nardo's cell while they were technically still boyfriend and girlfriend—low as hell on the totem pole and replaceable.

I was biting my lip, my leg was shaking uncontrollably, and my stomach was turning up in knots that were so vicious I thought I was about to miscarry. Nardo was doing more than embarrassing me in front of people, and it was stressing me out. I could not understand how we got so detached from one another for me to feel so inferior and low. This man was physically making me sick.

Holding my cell phone as close to my ear as it could go, I was trying to hone in on all the voices in the background in hopes that I would not hear Izzi's. Him finding out I was carrying another one of Nardo's babies would definitely put a stop to our creep sessions. I could not reveal the truth to Izzi until I knew this baby's fate. And I wouldn't know this baby's fate until Nardo and I could have a grown-up conversation.

Hanging up the phone, I dropped it into my lap then pulled away from the curb without even checking my mirrors. My carelessness caused nothing but chaos and confusion as a slew of horns sounded off and cars swerved from colliding with me and other cars that were in traffic. My only concern was getting to the trap house. I was not planning on letting my foot up off the gas pedal until I was on Dexter Avenue.

When I finally pulled up on the block, it was like time came to an eerie standstill. Everyone ceased all transactions and gawked with amazement as I stepped out of the car. They might have been shocked to see me, but I was embarrassed to stand in front of them not knowing if Nardo had already said I was trying to trap him with another kid. Still and all, though, I stood with my head up. I had on the "woman beater" shades, of course, mainly because my eyes were bloodshot from the tears, but they did add to my "Negro, I ain't to be fucked with" look.

Infuriated, I slammed my car door then took notice of Izzi, who was coming out of the spot. Even though he couldn't see the hurt in my eyes to know that something was seriously wrong, he just shook his head with disappointment. I'd just made love to him, and here I was back chasing Nardo, behaving like he and I didn't matter at all.

Sorry, Izzi, but I gotta do it!

It took an eternity to reach Renard. He was driving a Black Range Rover. JACK-ME was what the plate read. Whose it was I didn't know, and trust I didn't care. Spice, that braid-wearing floozy, sat posted in the passenger's seat, looking at me as if I were the devil himself.

Ain't this about a bitch. I mentally came to grips with what I was seeing.

I could see her ugly son tugging at my baby daddy's arm, probably anxious to get moving. I absorbed the entire atmosphere as my daughter's father set me on fire with his eyes. Knowing Renard's two-timing, two-faced, low-down, backstabbing behind would come to Spice's rescue if I tried to buck with her, my moves had to be carefully planned. Time just was not in my favor, so whatever jumped off from this point on was just fate.

"What the fuck is your purpose for being over here?" He tried clowning me as if our phone conversation had gone in one ear and out the other.

"Don't play stupid. You know what the hell was just said to you about fifteen minutes ago. You gonna act dumb?" I zoned out, starting to get bouncy and amped up. He was pissing me off, trying to stunt in front of Spice and his petty workers.

"Get the fuck on, Z. I'm warning you," he vehemently shouted, starting to open the car door as if I felt threatened.

If we scrapped, this would just be a cheap abortion.

"Don't get out, Nardo. Let's just go. She ain't even worth this bullshit. My son is in the ride too, and I don't want him around this hood garbage," Spice urged, trying to pull Nardo back in the car, but he was not having it.

"Back up, Spice. Let me handle this." He brushed her hand off his shoulder.

"Shut up, ho! This don't have nothing to do with you. This right here . . ." I said, arrogantly pointing at both me and Nardo with my face twisted and my eyes bucked. "This is between me and him, this nothing-ass fool." I placed my index finger to Nardo's forehead and pushed. "And as for your son, fuck him too," I disrespected recklessly. I was on track to make my way around to her side of the truck and smack the chick so me and her could get it in.

The entire neighborhood gathered as Nardo yoked me up quickly by my throat, body-slamming me onto the hood of an abandoned car. "You ain't nothing but trouble, Z. You been acting so childish, so bitter, and so petty, like a little piece of trash," he judged harshly.

"Fuck you, Nardo. Trash, my ass. Was I trash when your dirty dick was all up in me making kids, huh? Was I trash then, nigga?"

He tightened his grip on me. "Naw, Zaria, it's been fuck you! You're just easy pussy, that's all. You's a good-for-nothing, begging, vindictive slut! I done told you before, and this is the final time. Stay the hell away from my new family. Ain't shit I can do for ya anymore. Just let me go!" He released his hands from my now sore frame and began straightening his clothes.

"You're gonna regret you ever messed over me with yo' punk ass. Trust that. And that's my word," was the only thing I had left to say to Cidney's father. In my book, he was already dead. Every move I made from now on would be constructed to fuck Nardo's life up for the worse.

Nardo walking away toward Izzi, who was calling his name to get off me the entire time, gave me the window of opportunity I needed. Running up, I pounced in the truck, quickly letting one off in Spice's jaw. Yanking her by those tacky braids, I rammed her forehead into the dashboard three or four good times. Before I could really beat her ass again, like at Kimmie's, Nardo was dragging me out of the truck by my ankles. I was kicking and screaming.

"Get up off me, dude! I'm about to take this money-hungry tramp out the game once and for all," I heard him say to Izzi as he was trying to pull him away from the truck and off me. "Loose me, nigga." His words were firm.

"Watch yo' muthafuckin' mouth, guy, for real. This right here done went on long enough." Izzi made his presence felt. "Let her go."

"What?" Nardo redirected his rage, getting into Izzi's face. "You putting yo' dick in her or something? Why you so concerned?"

I was frozen solid. I didn't know if Izzi was going to blow our cover that we felt something between each other, but he'd already shown there was something strange going on by being so damned concerned about how Renard was treating me. I was low key geeked because now I knew I was more than a quick piece of ass to him. He was defending me. I blanked out and couldn't hear the words they were exchanging. There was just a ton of commotion on the block, and guys were picking who they were going to stand behind. Loyalty was really showing its true colors on Dexter.

I suddenly shrieked out in distress as I caught a swift punch to my stomach. "My baby! My baby!" I moaned, hugging my abdomen and bending over in agony.

Spice had hit me, and she'd hit me hard. I was stunned and defenseless, huddled over in so much pain I couldn't even defend myself. Payback was a bitch, and here I was feeling it firsthand. I saw the look on Izzi's face, and it was one of pure shock. He now knew I was pregnant too, and it dawned on me that things might change between us.

Fed up with his personal business being put out on the streets of Detroit, Nardo walked away from the approaching confrontation with Izzi. With complete contempt for me, Nardo spit in my face, telling me that was what I deserved for being a typical baby momma, before him and Spice got into the truck and pulled off. To add insult to injury, Spice let a solid round from Nardo's gun into the frame of my car before they pulled off the block.

"That stanking bitch." Her life was mine. What if Cidney was in the ride?

Nardo

My baby momma was pregnant again, and I knew the chances of it being mine were more than likely. I never strapped up when we had sex, and as of late I'd been busting in her on a regular. Now, I had to figure out a plan to get her to get rid of the kid. I barely wanted to be tied down to her with Cidney, and now I'd trapped myself with this unborn bastard.

"So, I guess you want me to accept the little fuck she claiming she's about to have, huh, Renard?" Spice assumed, interrupting my thoughts.

"Why don't you lay off right now? I got a lot on my mind, and you're just worrying about yourself," I snapped at her. I was getting bored with her being so self-absorbed. I was dealing with a lot of drama. What I couldn't seem to shake was the fact that Izzi had come to Zaria's defense. Where in the hell did he get off defending her when, to my knowledge, he couldn't stand the bitch? Things were really starting to come to light, and I didn't like what it brought out.

"I mean, damn, Renard. Being with you is so fucking complicated. I'm tired of the stuff your baby momma puts me through." Spice adjusted her body in the passenger's seat so she was facing me as I drove. "I know I took her man, but she's crazier than I expected, and no matter how much control you think you have, you really have none."

"Obviously not, Spice, because if I had even an ounce of control, you'd shut the hell up. I don't want to hear your mouth!"

"Oh, yeah, Renard! Is that right?"

"What part of that is you failing to understand?" I came back on her, pissed that she had enough audacity to even question me. I had love for Spice, but I couldn't tolerate mouth from no chick I messed with. She was becoming as bitchy as Zaria, and the main culprit behind Spice's reformation was Z.

"Whatever, boy!"

"Dig dis! You knew I had a girl before you laid down and gave me some. Now, I left her; not all because of you, but nevertheless, I did leave her. Now she's pregnant. Okay, you can't act as if you didn't know I was still hitting that. That's reality. You didn't get me fair, and if you ever lose me, you won't lose me fair either. That's the deal you made and the chances you have to take—especially when you sleep with someone else's man."

"So, you gonna play me like that?" She bossed up, showing me her island gangster after getting a gigantic dose of realism smashed into her face.

"It ain't playing you if I'm giving you real talk. I'm letting you know the 411, and if you can't handle that official shit, then I can't help you." I rubbed my beard repeatedly, which was a habit I had when I was frustrated or had a lot on my mind. "But point blank, Matilda Lynn," I said, using her government name to really get her hyped, "I'm tired of always hearing about poor, misunderstood you. You're just as much to blame as me."

"Oh, so let me get this straight. Now I'm the reason your supposed-to-be baby's mother pulled out my hair at the nail shop?" she dumbly questioned, throwing the insult back in my lap. "And just put this lump on my head? Is that what you telling me?"

"Yeah, if you wouldn't have been running off at the mouth, she wouldn't have known we had a secret thing going on, so that's on you!"

"Nigga, if you were as tough and cocky as you sit here professing, then you should've told her you had a li'l somethin'-somethin' on the side instead of letting her insinuate it. Every man wanna be a pimp," she said, turning all the way in her seat, getting louder.

"Ha ha! And every tropical island homewrecker wants their cheating man to be faithful," I mocked her before she slapped me upside the head.

The truck swerved, and I instantly slammed down on the brakes. Reaching over, I wrapped my hands firmly around Spice's throat. "Don't ever fuckin' disrespect me like that!" I released the tramp because her son started to cry. She was now boo-hooin' too, but I didn't care. It was too freaking late! She shouldn't have put her hands on a playa. Spice got what she deserved once again for that mouth of hers!

"Matter of fact, don't say shit else until I tell ya to. If you got something else to say, raise yo' damn hand! You done fucked around, making yo' position slip."

She looked at me as if she couldn't believe the words coming out of my mouth. Spice could suck my dick at this point. If she couldn't take the heat, she would have to bounce. My main agenda was to get Zaria to get rid of that baby.

Izzi

I started shoving an out-of-breath Zaria up against her car, not giving a fuck if I hurt her more than she already was. Here I was giving her this good dick and falling for that ass, and she was over here set-tripping on Nardo.

"So, you keeping his kid or what?" I turned her around, lifting her face to lock eye contact.

"Dawg, I can't even believe you wanna sit here and question me about that after all that shit just went down. And to top it off, you almost blew our dang-gone cover," she answered, starting to stare around in a panic. "Matter of fact," Zaria continued, "I ain't even got time to sit here and explain myself. That silly ho just left holes in my ride, and I'm about to get even." She rubbed her stomach to ease the pain.

Zaria was trying hard to get my grip loose from her waist, but I was holding on tightly. Honey was fine as hell, but so damn dumb! She couldn't see that my manz ain't give a fuck about her, 'cause if he did, none of this would be going down. And for damn sure ol' girl Spice would've been on the pavement for letting out a round into her car. The more I looked at Zaria, the angrier I got. I wanted to just punch her dead in the belly like Spice had. Here she was carrying that punk nigga's child when I really wanted my seed up in that.

"Damn, Izzi. Let the fuck go. I gotta bounce for real, and this ain't even the place for us to be showing public affection," she said, snapping me back into reality.

"Why the hell don't you just let go?" I argued, not really expecting a response. "You don't know how pathetic you look chasing behind him like a lost little puppy. A real man was trying to show you respect, but you like being treated like a shitbag. So, go."

Okay, do you think that girl cared what I just said? Hell fuck naw! She didn't even blink an eye at my remarks. Zaria just got in her car, started the ignition, and sped the hell off. I was done with her ass. To hell with getting tangled into her messy world. I had already shown too much when I fronted Nardo on her behalf.

Nardo

After I cooled down and thought about it, I called my baby momma to see where her head was at. That pregnancy crap she blurted out had me messed up in the head, but knowing Zaria the way I did, it was probably all a huge, fantastic, concocted lie. She didn't answer, so I left a voice mail for her to get back at me. Spice was heated and sat her insecure ass quiet in the passenger's seat. I heard her smack her lips several times, and I was ready to spit in her face, but I held off.

We never made it out that night. I just dropped her and her son off and headed back to the block to pick up my money and speak to my dude Izzi about his Captain Save-a-Ho actions earlier.

CHAPTER THIRTEEN

Zaria

I saw Nardo's ass calling me, but I didn't know what the heck for. I didn't have time for his drama prevention or his sorry excuses. He should've laid that trick Spice the fuck out for even thinking she could lay hands on me. I was beyond tired of him letting hoes who he didn't even have a real history with come between us, especially now that we had Cidney. I'd really hyped myself up to think she would complete us as a family. If nothing else, I felt I'd get more loyalty as the mother of his child.

My voice mail alert went off, but I didn't even bother to check it. I was not answering the phone until my truth was out, his lies were exposed, and vengeance was mine.

Izzi had pissed me off too. Though he was hung like a horse and could stroke me to sleep, he and I weren't official with one another, and he couldn't make a claim on me publicly—which meant he should not be twisted all up in his feelings for me as deeply as he was. It was not like me and Nardo's relationship was hidden, or my intent to keep fuckin' around with my baby daddy was concealed. Izzi's knowledge of the truth didn't match up with how he'd reacted; and real talk, I was still shocked.

I called and arranged with the babysitter that I would pay her in advance if she could keep Cidney for a couple of days, and she was game. Little mama was broke and needed the cash anyway. I told her I would be around the way in a few hours with Cid's things and the money and to hold tight until then.

I caught a cab to a car rental company and walked out of there with a black Ford Fusion with a sun roof. Now I had to ditch my car. It was no way I could be riding a whip with bullet holes and shit. I just left my shot-up shit on the streets. I didn't even care if they towed it because I planned on reporting it stolen later anyway. I couldn't try to get any insurance money or even report Spice to the boys in blue because I was going to retaliate on that homewrecker in the worst way, and I didn't need any extra leads heading my way. It was now time to really set my plan into motion.

"Q Nails, this Kimmie."

"What's up, Kim? This is Zaria. I know the shop is banging, but I need your services ASAP."

"What time you want come, since you in such rush?" she asked, being her regular, nosy self. "Sue Lee busy, but I will get her to make time for you. You good customer, plus Kimmie know you got gossip."

"That's a good look, girl. I'll be there tonight at eight."

"You come on time. Me ain't trying to be in this beech all night, Z gurl, and I don't want to hear Sue Lee mouth, okay? Good-bye." Her rude Korean ass hung up on me with a quickness.

I headed in the direction of home and turned up WJLB to hear JAY-Z's old-school song "Cry." That shit was back in the day as hell, but no doubt still relevant.

"Once a good girl gone bad, she's gone forever."

Nardo had called my phone two more times before I reached home, and I still hadn't answered. It was not nothing he could say to me on the real. I parked a few houses down so he would think I was not home, just in case he pulled a pop-up. He didn't know this car, but I had to cover all bases with his slick behind.

First thing on my agenda was to get Cidney together some clothes. I wanted to keep my baby girl with me because I missed her so much, but I didn't want her caught up in this bullshit her father was putting me through. True enough, I could've walked away, but it was not that simple. Me and Nardo had almost two long years together, and that made history that can't be easily forgotten.

As I was pulling footies and pajamas out of the drawer, her baby book caught my eye. Of course, I took it out and began to reminisce. She had gotten so big, and I was already starting to miss the days I had first brought her home, when everything was so peachy between me and Nardo.

"Dang, can a chick relax without people constantly bothering me?" I shrieked when I heard the house phone ring.

It was as if I could never have a moment to myself. I dragged my feet getting to the phone. I really didn't want to be bothered, but it could have been the sitter about my watching my child. I snatched up the phone and checked the caller ID.

Wayne County Jail! What the fuck!

"Hello," I answered impatiently.

"You have a collect call from . . ." said the recording, and then I heard that ho's name. "Melanie McGee." I hung up quick, fast, and in a hurry. I didn't know what that tramp was calling my house for. I couldn't do shit for her but stick my foot up her ass. With all the things that had taken place, I had forgotten to go press charges against her. They had to be holding her for something else, because she should've been back on the streets to fuck another girl's man by now.

I had slow-stepped on that whole situation. The answering machine said I had twelve messages, and I thought they were all bill collectors because no one really had this number, but I decided to check them anyhow.

The first one said, "Zaria, this is Melanie. Please pick up. We need to talk. I know shit is fucked up between us but on the real, we need to get back at Nardo."

The second one was her too. "Yeah, you was wrong for taking my man, but that's the nature of the hood. Let's put beef aside. Z, please pick up."

She had left a third one: "Zaria! Zaria! Are you there? . . . All right, if you don't want to talk, then fuck it. You know I haven't always been an ass-kisser, but I'm caught up. He left you for dead just like me for that other hoe!"

It was her fourth message that made me grab Cid's clothes and rush out of the house.

Melanie

Zaria's mean-spirited ass had picked up that time, but she hung up obviously when she heard it was me calling. I was sitting in the pokey for an outstanding warrant I had for a raid I was busted in on the corner of Waverly and Dexter. I ran in OPI Nails and hid, but some punk ass gave up my name and info too. The cops didn't make a big deal on it, but of course, when they caught me up, it was all of a sudden breaking news.

I was out of options. Nardo had left me there to rot and burn in jail. I had to call somebody to help me. All that I'd been through with that loser, it was more than clear now that I was just a good piece of ass to him. Well, hell, maybe it was not even that good to him, because if it was, he would've been down there to save my black behind.

Zaria had pissed me off, coming to my house and tearing up my crib like that. I thought I had an up on her by calling and letting her hear firsthand that her man was fucking me, but she showed a total breech of respect by riding to where I laid my head. So, no doubt I had to retaliate by going to her spot.

When I had pulled up to her suburban house and saw the Camaro sitting in the driveway, it infuriated me, because I realized it was all thanks to Nardo and his dope-selling life. Before I even rang the doorbell, I peeped in the window, seeing her house was laid with flat screens, plush carpet, and the furniture you only saw in Art Van, not that rinky-dinky, hand-me-down crap I was subjected to purchasing from the flea market. Here she was living lavish, and I was a pitiful, bona fide gold digger, barely making it from day to day. This female was now living my life!

The old woman who'd watched Zaria tear my shit up called the landlord that night. I had already pulled one out of my sleeve to stay there after I had an eviction notice taped to my door a month before. That time, I had to let him feel me up plus come out my pocket with the little $300 savings I had left. So, with the events Zaria's ass had put me through, I had to deep throat and swallow, not to mention let him fuck me just to let me keep a roof over my head.

Zaria had not only stolen my meal ticket, but because of her, I was degrading myself just so the little stuff I had wouldn't be thrown out on the curb. Just thinking about all of that made me nut up even worse when she pranced her behind down the carpeted staircase in her silk designer print robe. I swear I wanted to cut the man-stealer's neck off.

As I lay back on my stinking cot, my eyes burned with spiteful tears. I was so tired of being a little nothing with nothing to live for but the next chick's man. I gave it up to anyone who offered a few bucks, and I swore I was in love, but I knew deep down inside I was just looking for someone to actually care about me—which they wouldn't.

Damn, I need to change my life!

No sooner than I got ready to try to sleep off some of this time until the police figured out what to do with my ass, a little cocky female police detective came to open my cell.

"Melanie McGee . . ."

CHAPTER FOURTEEN

Nardo

"Where's my muthafuckin' money, nigga?" The little corner hustler already owed me for a sack I'd left him a few days ago, and lately there had been a lot of excuses.

"Nardo, give me a few more hours to get it together. I ain't sold the whole thang yet," he said, trying to bargain with me.

"Listen, guy, ain't shit this way stupid. Run my money or pay with your life, and that's my word!" Just as I'd predicted, dude took a cop, stuttering and slow-slurring his sentences. I was not trying to hear nothing he was saying. I was tired of taking shorts from these punks. I didn't have this problem on the west side. These low-quality hustlers on this side of town were always full of fairy-tale lies.

Izzi wanted me to help him lock down the east, and yeah, I felt him. They were over here getting straight buck wild with the package, and they most definitely needed a thick wooden bat upside their craniums. I instinctively pulled out my piece, pressing the cold silver steel onto the side of his left temple.

"You think I'm gonna put my word on a basehead? I know you smokin'," I alleged, getting louder.

By now the entire block was coming back out of their houses to catch another show starring me. I was being extra hard because I was forced to. Just a few short hours ago, shit had gone berserk between me and my baby momma. I had to let the hood know, young and old, that I hadn't lost control of any situations.

"Come on, Nardo. Please, man. I ain't smoking no more. Please, I got kids at home and mouths to feed." He pleaded for his life. "Just give me another day or two."

I slid my burner back into the waistband of my pants, deciding I was not gonna catch no case on this fool. He just needed a *Scared Straight* tactic. I had no choice. I did go upside his head a few times with my fist, and when he landed on the ground, I kicked his fragile, bag-of-bones body. "Nate, I want my money tonight, or for real for real, you can lay out your casket clothes ahead of time." I walked away, feeling vindicated in front of the hood.

"I see you can't keep yo' shit low key all of a sudden, with baby momma pop-ups and drama on the block with these heads. Niggas over here trying to make their money, and you're setting the spot on fire." Izzi grimed me as I walked on the porch of our spot.

"You and Z fuckin' around, dawg, or what?" I accused him, getting straight to the point.

"You playing me real close. But right about now, why you even care what I might've done? Last I checked, you ain't give a fuck." He lit the blunt in his hand, obviously throwing up our conversation we had on the way to the club. "What? Now you do?"

"Yeah, well, even if I didn't, that was not an all clear to bang my baby momma."

"Look, Nardo, we got money on the streets and heavy weight to throw around. Now, you can keep dwelling on this bullshit, or get straight to business. But whatever the case, I'm gonna get mine. I ain't got time for no broads, least of all yours."

"I'm with that most def, but I still ain't trying to hear on the streets that you hard-dicking her." I swole up, staring him dead in the eyes, but he didn't even seem shook. "Zaria is off limits! Ya feel me?" We were standing toe to toe.

"Call it what it is, Nardo, but don't come at me with no shit unless it got to do with gettin' that bread."

"Well, we'll get that dough till it plays out. Let's roll and set up shop." I came back to my senses as I started walking to the truck. "I don't know why I'm bugging out. We better than that anyway."

Me and Izzi got in my truck and headed toward the east side location where we'd cook up at. Izzi's great aunt's senior citizen's apartment was the perfect place. We played it off like we were going to visit, but low key we had our empire in there. No one even knew this spot existed, except for us two and her.

Auntie Eva was very well taken care of, and we always looked out for her friends in there also. Shit, old folks need money and love too, and we provided that for her. She wanted for nothing.

CHAPTER FIFTEEN

Zaria

I sat in the parking lot, waiting on Melanie to walk out of the county jail. I had let a thousand fall out my pocket for her freedom. She owed me big time, and I was gonna straight use her. Yeah, I fucked Nardo right out of her arms, but before all that, we were thick as thieves. I didn't care how hurt or betrayed she felt sitting behind those cell walls. I was not down for a bitch coming to my house or calling my phone, trying to play me like a fool. She was about to learn a lesson.

"Excuse me, miss lady, can I have a few dollars for a burger and a cup of coffee?" A bum eased up as I stepped out of the car so Melanie could see me.

"Naw, I ain't even got it to spare," I shot back, giving a cold stare to the front. I couldn't stand people asking for my goddamn money. Now, if you want to pick the trash up around my house or do some extracurricular tasks, then I could hook you up and pay for your time, but free change? Fuck naw! That was why when Melanie stepped foot out of lockup, she was gonna work that G off, whether she wanted to or not!

Melanie

"You've made bond," the officer announced.

I could've sworn she was coming to take me for some more questioning about the events that had went down at Zaria's house, but obviously, Nardo had come to his senses and was about to bail me out.

"Damn, he made a sister wait it out," I nonchalantly mentioned to the officer, trying to make conversation as we took our walk from the cell.

She didn't say a single, solitary word to me. I guess she thought she was something extra special because she had a gun or some crap like that, but whatever it was, at least I was outta that joint.

Forgetting about my so-called life change I'd vowed to make, I was angry once I was back on the street. Nardo was gonna hear my mouth about making me wait, but first I had to re-pussy-whip this fool 'cause he done lost his mind, thinking he could have me sit up like some caged bird. Anyways, I couldn't wait to get out and get back to my house and soak in a hot-ass bath. The jail smell was awful. I smelt my damn self!

Zaria

Melanie came out of the jail looking just like she always looked to me: rough, raggedy, and tore up from the floor up. Of course, they made her take her hair down and take the strings out of her sneakers. Mel thought she could roll with any big dog, but low key, she couldn't hang with the broads in the county jail.

I locked my eyes onto her and was staring hard. I was prepared to scrap with her right outside of the jail if need be. That's how pissed I was. Our eyes met each other, and that was it.

"Awwww, hell naw! So, you posted a bitch's bond! You dumb as I thought you were," she said, walking toward me. "You dropped a grand to see my pretty ass?"

"Naw, not dumb, homegirl, but pissed off. What box of tough cookies did you swallow that had you geeked up like Jeezy to come to my crib?" I questioned, walking up to meet her with a clenched fist.

"Excuse me, ma'am, do you have some loose change that you can spare?" the bum asked Melanie before she could even get back with me.

"Naw, I ain't got a dime for ya. Besides, didn't you just see me get out?" she screamed at the begging man then turned her attention back on me. "And as for you, Zaria, I ain't had nothing but bread and water in this piece, and I'm still ready to fuck you up," she yelled.

"You so freaking stupid, Melanie. Let me clue you in on a few things. Nardo left you for me and only hooked up with you behind my back. He still doesn't claim you and will never want you. Isn't it obvious, since he left you up in jail with murderers, thieves, and whatever other lunatic that's lurking up in there? What's wrong with you?" I asked, talking patiently, wanting to bring her self-esteem down to a pulp. "And dang gee, yo' breath stank like the sewer!"

Melanie covered her mouth shamefully as she spoke. "Nardo might've left me for you, but he still kept creeping back. Now, what does that say? Hmmm, to me that says your cat ain't shit, and I got that comeback."

"Well, you ain't shit but some pussy," I said, raising my voice. She was aggravating me once again. I was mad bitter that Nardo kept backtracking with her. That gave her a little leverage on me and some truth to hit me with. "Don't think for one second that I won't beat the mess out of you. This right here, baby girl, is not a game. I have never been sloppy nothing. He left you in the gutter. He chose me," I proudly stated like Nardo was a crown prince.

"First of all, you ain't gonna lay one finger on me. Second, this right here"—She laughed, mocking me—"is a game. If it was not, you wouldn't have bailed out the female he was cheating on you with for the whole relationship. And lastly, *most importantly*, he chose the next ho, not you, and definitely not me. So, what dream world are you living in?"

"You got some nerve, Mel!"

"Excuse me, excuse me!" the bum interjected once more, interrupting our argument.

"What!" we screamed in unison at him.

This guy was ticking me off. Why couldn't he just move on down the street to bother some other suckers willing to give their change up for a blow?

"Please spare me some change," he begged like begging was going out of style.

"Don't you see I'm in the middle of getting ready to beat this tramp down?" I asked him seriously, waiting for an answer.

"Yeah, okay, act like it, slut. You must want this grungy bum to see me lay you out. And who would give a rat's ass if they locked me back up?" Mel boldly blew out her mouth, really feeling herself.

The bum then got cocky, having had enough of getting insulted as if he was not even standing there.

"Naw, y'all dumb, cheap, no-spare-change-having bitches! What I see is that a real pimp is playing y'all both to the middle, getting pussy and respect all the way. He really got that power. Where he at? Maybe that kingpin got some change to spare," he mumbled walking away, damn near falling off the curb.

Me and Mel were left standing there dumbfounded. His dirty ass had went off on us, and to make matters worse, he was telling the truth. We were once aces, and dick had torn us apart. Because of Renard, she had threatened my life, and I was coming to mash her head in front of the county jail. It was what it was! That nigga really was pimpin' our asses.

"Look, I appreciate you getting me out of the pokey, but if your scary ass wouldn't have stolen my man and called the po-po, I wouldn't have been in there anyway."

"No matter what a woman of my caliber does for you, it's always our fault you fucked up." I was condescending and agitated by her pathetic ways.

"You know you started all this junk. But let's just call a truce. Nardo is the real target here, like the bum just said. He was playing both sides to the middle," she responded. "We could just go back to being friends."

"I really don't have time for childish stuff, Melanie. I have Cidney, a hurt heart, and most importantly, I have unfinished business with my baby daddy and his mistress. I bailed you out, not because I missed our friendship; because a female's truce don't mean shit to a hungry mouth or an empty pocket. I bailed you out to beat your ass down, but now I could use you in my plan to bring Nardo on his knees," I said to her, basically ignoring that she wanted to be aces again. "You with it or what?"

"I'm down for whatever, but I don't want revenge because of you. Nardo crossed me too."

"Yeah, act like it, Mel. I'm out for self. You can do whatever you want *after* you follow my rules."

She smacked her lips. I knew she couldn't stand that I was in control, but I had her right where I wanted her. Mel had no idea that I truly did miss how we would hang back in the day, but I couldn't trust anyone, so I had to play the role.

After a few brief moments of scheming, we jumped in the car. I had to get to Kimmie's cousin Sue Lee quick. In between her and Kimmie talking shit to me about their time, I'd have two more enemies in the streets.

As time ticked by, I was itching more and more to ask her just how her and my daughter's father had hooked back up. I know that whole saying about never ask what you can't handle or what you really don't want to know, but fuck a rule.

"So, how long after me and Nardo linked up did y'all start on the sneak tip?" I inquired, tapping my nails on the steering wheel as I hit the freeway.

"Let's get something straight, Zaria. Me and him were never sneaking. He was mine first. Remember when you decided to break the code? But to answer your question: honestly, we never really stopped. Things were off and on at times, but never completely off. He always used to say he couldn't stop messing with you because you looked out for him when we were kids." Melanie sat in the passenger's seat, smirking.

I knew she wasn't lying over what she'd said. Nardo had to tell her how my parents looked out with the knowledge he capitalized on.

"You're dirty as shit, Mel. Calling my phone with that drama, messing with him while I was pregnant."

"Oh, and you're just the goddamn friendly fairy," she said, cutting me off in mid-sentence. "Your brain must be frozen solid, or you're just stuck on stupid. He was mine *first*, so that makes him your sloppy seconds."

"Hmph. Yeah, does it appear that I'm second to you?" I hesitantly conceded, turning the radio up.

I was not even trying to make her a priority. I had to get my game straight for Renard. I couldn't do anything but laugh at the whole situation in my mind. Here we were, letting a Negro come between our childhood friendship, all because I was status and money hungry. And then that fool Nardo had the audacity to leave me and her both hanging out to dry for the next bitch. How did this happen? Who did Renard think he was?

There was now an unspoken understanding between me and Melanie that we would bond for at least a short time, in order to pay Nardo back. She was cool in the past, but on the real, I think we'd gone too far to even go back to being all buddy-buddy.

"So, how's Cidney?" Melanie genuinely seemed concerned, trying to make small talk and help break the tension inside the car.

"First, take this Tic Tac. Then we'll talk!" I clowned her.

It was actually good to catch up on old times, seeing as how I really didn't have any female friends except for Kimmie. We kicked it back and forth for a while until we pulled up in front of the shop.

When we stepped out of the car, Kimmie's slanted-eye expression was priceless. I knew she was going to be talking mad ying-yang. I just hoped I could understand her crazy ass when she got going, mixing two languages into one. Kimmie always had me rolling.

Started from the bottom now we're here.

My cell had kept ringing that song the entire ride from the jail.

"What, nigga?" I answered the phone screaming, knowing that Nardo was wanting nothing but drama. I was tired of him blowing up my shit.

"Baby girl, I know you're pissed off, but chill out so we can talk," he blurted out as if nothing had just happened.

"Now you wanna talk to me, Nardo? I tried that tolerant game with you *before* you yoked me up in front of your crew of losers and *before* you let Spice put her hands on me and shoot up my car. I know for a fact you don't think talking is going to solve the problems you've created. Or are you really that stupid?"

Nardo was quiet, and I was done with the pointless conversation. "Now, if you'll excuse me, I'm busy at the moment. And P.S., stop calling my fucking phone!"

Both Kimmie and Mel were all in my mouth.

"Okay, chick, I need my nails soaked off, and then Sue Lee can get to my Beyoncé-type sew-in." I got straight to the point, hoping I'd distracted her from the phone call.

I really didn't want to go into detail with either one of them about my conversation with Nardo. Had I been on my toes, I wouldn't have said anything about the fight or the bullets Spice let out, but I was still furious, so it slipped. Kimmie couldn't wait for me to get into her shop.

"Me not stupid, Z gurl. Nardo kick you ass?" she inquired, locking the door after me and Melanie walked in. "And what thee fuck! You and this thang here friend now or what? Hell must freeze over. Me not know this shit."

"It's a long story, Kimmie, but I really need for you to move your feet and get at me A-one. I have things to do. Where is Sue Lee? Eating rice?"

"Kimmie make time for you nails and make cousin squeeze you in, and you get the smart mouth. Oh, no. You not respect the game, Z gurl," she scolded, shaking her head, walking toward the back area where Sue Lee was perched, eating a huge bowl of white rice, just like I thought.

"Hey, dirty one who smell like hot fire shit on stick! You broke ass get nail done too?" She dogged out Melanie, who, real talk, truly did need a bath badly. "You pay first. I know you type. Full set and run!"

"Dang, Kimmie, you just don't know when to stop, do you? News flash: this is America. You ain't nobody over here!" Mel retorted, apparently pissed that she'd called her out. "I used to be one of your best clients back in the day."

"Yeah, but that day long gone." Kimmie snapped her fingers. "Long, long gone!"

"You bitch!" Melanie acted like she was ready to swing on Kimmie.

"Oh, fuck this, Z gurl! You bring drama back to Kimmie shop." She twisted her upper lip, waving that nail file at me. "That stinky gurl talk crazy talk! Her sick in head!"

"Okay, y'all, let's just chill out. Kimmie, you were wrong for coming on Mel like that, but anyway, just squash it so I can get my shit right." I had become the instant peacemaker.

Kimmie sucked her teeth, and Melanie walked away to sit in the waiting room.

"Yeah, you sit stink ass over there!" Frowning, Kimmie sprayed almost the entire can of air freshener.

"Fuck you, Kimmie, and your raw-cat-eating ass!"

I couldn't blame Mel for being upset with Kimmie. She was blunt and didn't care how you took it, but I was not getting ready to side up totally with Melanie. We might've resolved the issues momentarily, but I was not her best friend by a damn sight.

"You sit down right here in chair and explain. Kimmie don't like to not know gossip."

"Yeah, all right," I replied, taking a seat.

She couldn't believe that Nardo had actually let Spice shoot up my car and fight me. Yet, it was not unbelievable to her that he had put his hands on me. He'd done that several prior times, which forced me to wear my celebrity shades to hide my bruises.

"So, how you come to be back friends with that ugly-faced troublemaker?" Kimmie shot Mel the true evil eye.

"She called my house and left a few messages. I bailed her out to kick her ass, and out of some magic, we squashed the beef. She wants revenge on Nardo just like me, and I might as well use her as a pawn. I plan on doing some real scandalous stuff in a few days, and she'd be a perfect candidate to take the fall."

"Ooh, you sooooo clever, Z gurl. You get her," she whispered, amused. "I like plan already!"

A few hours later, Sue Lee had finished my hair, and my nails were soaked off. I had Kimmie do a manicure on my natural nails. I didn't need any glamorous curves to do my dirty work, and I sure was not trying to have them break, either. I didn't care what bullshit I went through; my appearance meant the world to me. A bitch would never catch me slipping.

After we were done with the whole makeover event, I took Melanie past her house to grab some clothes and wash her filthy ass. I couldn't take her smell any longer. Of course, I waited in the car. After that, we went to check in at the Doubletree across the street from Fairlane Mall. I was not going to be staying at my house for a while. I needed peace and quiet and a place where Nardo couldn't find me.

As for Melanie, she had no idea what I really had in store for her. She was having a good day. I'd posted her bond, and now she was benefiting from the luxury of her own room in a hotel. Just being geeked to be able to hang with me was enough to cloud her dimwitted brain. *Poor, dumb bitch!*

CHAPTER SIXTEEN

Nardo

I'd been calling Zaria all day, and she was shooting me straight to voice mail. I was starting to really get pissed off that she was playing me to the left. I rode past the house but didn't see her car or any other sign of life. I thought about calling her mother's house to at least see if Cidney was over there, but I was not in the mood for all her mom's "I'm tired of y'all's bullshit" speech.

"This ho got the game twisted!" I fumed, slamming down Auntie's phone on the hard wood table.

Izzi was sitting across from me, bagging product. He glanced up, shook his head, and then looked back down to concentrate on what he was doing.

"All right, so I got all the weight from the last package set up in the spots on the east. We need to take some bread out the stash and meet up with the connect again to get the west pumpin' real good." Izzi was focused on business.

"Naw, we'll keep the east for profit and flip that into product. The west will just have to wait it out a while. No sense in overbidding our shit." I let him know how I felt.

"Fuck that, man. You always playing that slow role. Hit 'em and hit 'em hard! I can't stand all that fall back garbage!"

"Izzi, you try and run up on brothers putting in work in their territory with no strategy or plan. Shiiiit, that's how empires come down and dudes get killed."

"Well, when I see a weak set of fools, my job is to put them out of their misery."

"Damn, cuzzo. Slow yo' roll! Let's just hold off a few days at least and meet with our soldiers. Stop making all these irrational-ass decisions. We'll rule the D in due time."

Izzi didn't bother to come back on me because his cell rang.

"What up, ma?" He questioned the person on the other end with a soft-spoken tone.

After he got off the phone, he informed me about a wild party a few strippers he dealt with were throwing at All-Stars. That was what I was talking about. I was down for some ass shaking, so I let him know we could roll out together. Fuck Zaria, Melanie, and Spice!

Izzi

I was tired of Nardo thinking he could make all the decisions and kick back. I was trying to make money hand over fist. Who in the fuck did he think he was?

I'd already monopolized the east side, while he was dancing around with only a few spots on the west. Soldiers on the street were starting to see who the true boss was, and that was proving to be me.

While Nardo was preoccupied, getting so caught up in baby momma drama and stank hood pussy, I was demanding respect and planning on his demise. Hell, deep-dicking Zaria was just an added bonus. And besides, I'd messed around and caught feelings in the process. We were in the middle of kicking it about adding more spots on the west when Zaria called my phone.

"What up, ma?" I smiled, answering the phone on the first ring, happy to hear her voice. "Where you been hiding out at?"

"A whole lot you already know. Are you around Nardo?" she asked.

"Yeah, ma. Ya know I keeps it on the grind. What ya need?" I said, letting her know and keeping it low key in front of her baby daddy. I didn't need that lame getting even more suspect.

"Well, I need to talk to you in private, maybe at our spot," she said, giving my manhood an instant boost, thinking I could hit it again. Make-up sex was known to get a brother a lot of special oral attention.

"Yeah, that's what's up. What time is the set up?"

"Come as soon as possible, sooner than later, but do me a quick favor and make sure Nardo be busy later on tonight. I'll explain when I see you. And, baby, I'm sorry," she ended before hanging up.

"Yeah, see yo' hot ass there," I spoke to no one, still wanting to play the shit off.

I knew Nardo was ear hustling, and I had to come up with a something since Zaria wanted me to occupy him later. I wondered what that was all about, but I knew I would soon find out. Knowing her, at this point, it had to be something wild that I'd probably end up regretting.

A chick I used to mess around with was a dancer, and she'd told me earlier about the set they were throwing, but I was not gonna deal with Nardo on this one. It was perfect timing for Z, so to hell with it.

"Let's roll out to see some booty poppin' at All-Stars tonight," I suggested to Nardo. Things were a definite go from there.

Zaria

I pulled up at the Comfort Inn and decided to call Nardo back for the playoff. I glanced around the parking lot to see if I saw any familiar cars then decided to pull around to the back. As I was pulling into another parking spot, Nardo answered his phone.

"I see you can't stop calling. What do you want?" I blurted out when he picked up as I reclined my seat back.

"I think you done forgot who the fuck I am, girl! Pregnant or not, I will beat the hell out of you. Where you at, anyhow?"

"Boy, bye. You ain't in no position to call shots around here or question me. Now, I've been wasting time on this conversation too long, and you haven't even said what it is that you want so damn bad," I said, rubbing my face, getting impatient.

"I'll be by the house at ten, so you should make sure you are there too. I miss my baby girl."

"Nigga, please! I was born at night, but not last night. You don't miss Cidney. You just call yourself doing damage control. You don't want me to have this baby. I'm not stupid. And I'm just as pissed that your rotten-ass seed made it back up in me. Please believe that! You don't have to come around and play daddy to make me give it up. I'll stick a rusty hanger up my coochie before I breed for you again, ho!" I flipped my phone shut, smacking my lips.

This fool really thinks I'm stupid. Damn, how did I let him run over me so long? I questioned myself as I pulled down the mirror to check out how I was looking.

My lip gloss was still popping, so all I had to do was fix a few loose hairs. I leaned over, checking to make sure I had enough cash on hand to pay for the room. I didn't need any trails to my credit card. No one needed to know my whereabouts. I knew the attendant wouldn't ask for an ID if I tipped him an extra fifty. Money always made questions disappear.

I walked into the room, turning the air temperature on low. I flicked on the TV. One of my favorite movies, *All About the Benjamins*, was on. Mike Epps was in the convenience store mocking the clerk; it was the beginning. I pulled out my cell phone to call Izzi.

He needs to quit! I thought when I saw there were two missed calls from Nardo and one voice mail. Choosing to ignore them, I didn't return his calls. Dude would learn that I was not a fucking joke or a raggedy pair of house shoes.

"Talk to me," Izzi said, answering the phone.

"Hey, boo boo, it's room two twenty-five. I'm powering off my phone, so get here quick."

"Yeah, that's what's up. I'm en route shortly."

I could tell from the simple conversation he was taking care of business, so that was just protocol of being wifey to a street boy. I took off my clothes and got into the warm, steaming shower. I was still mad at Izzi for putting me on front, but my pussy was yearning for some attention, and I knew he'd be more than willing to answer the call. Besides, I knew I could manipulate him to do what I wanted with sex. He'd let it slip through his actions that he'd caught feelings for me, and in the state of mind I was in, that was a bad damn move. I didn't care about hurting anybody, as long as my revenge was played out.

I soon heard Izzi knock on the door as I was putting a little lotion on my skin. I wrapped the fluffy white towel around my damp body and went to the door. After glancing through the peephole to make sure it was him, I opened it, quickly turning around prancing back toward the bed. This was all a playoff game. When I saw him on the other side of the door, I wanted him right then. His hair was still braided tight, and he had on his signature wheat Timberlands, dark denim True Religion shorts, and a green-and-beige matching shirt. He thought he was still walking the streets of Brooklyn.

"What up, Z?" he greeted me, coming in and grabbing a sista from behind.

Twisting around, I gave him a long hug as I nibbled on his earlobe a little bit to arouse him. He ran his hands down my back until he gripped my ass firmly.

"You, baby," I cooed

"You come to your senses yet or what?" He yanked down on my weave, getting a little rougher with me. "I didn't like your attitude before."

"We'll talk about that later, Izzi. Just get between these legs and release some stress." I giggled, ignoring his question for the time being.

He laid me down on the bed and gave it to me just the way I liked it, and definitely the way I needed it. He was 'bout it and it made me be 'bout it right back. I gave him my best Jenna Jameson imitation fuck, not because I felt he needed it, but because I felt like if he came good and right, he would do anything I asked of him. After we finished sexing, we relaxed in the bed, legs entangled.

"So, Z, you ready to play my wifey or not?" The question made it seem like he was already pussy stroked. "You need to be housing my seed in that belly."

"Naw, not quite. I gotta tie things up with Nardo and take his ass down. A woman scorned is a bitter bitch." I let him in on my fury.

He fell out in laughter and got up to roll himself a blunt. "What the fuck you mean, take him down?"

"I mean tear his shit up, break up him and Spice, make him wish he never fucked me over and ran my name through the mud."

"Are you serious, girl?" he asked, gazing over at me as if I was funnier than those lames he'd seen on *Comic View*. "Are you?"

"So serious that I bonded Melanie out from jail and made amends with her punk ass."

"You lying!"

"Naw, Izzi. By the time my plan is played out, Mister Renard will have paid the ultimate price for doing me dirty."

"And you're confiding in me because you trust me, huh?" he asked, catching me off guard. "What makes you think I won't put my boy up on your little plan?"

"You ain't loyal to that nigga, Izzi, so let's just cut the bullshit and keep it boogie. You wouldn't be here with his baby momma if you were."

"Yeah, truth told. So, what part do you want me to play in this little game of yours?" he wondered, still laughing and not taking me seriously as he lit his blunt.

"Well, for starters, understand that everything I do with Nardo is for his downfall and my come-up only, not for me to be with him. So, unless I ask for your assistance, keep quiet and don't act all suspect around him. And tonight, keep him from going home to his li'l bachelor pad. That will be the first place I hit tonight."

"Girl, you crazy. I got yo' back, but you better slow up on that stupid shit. Nardo ain't tough tone to me, but that buster might be competition to you."

"All right, act like it. I ain't never scared!" We had to laugh at that one, but deep down, a bitch was serious.

After I put Izzi up on the rest my game plan for later, I crawled seductively across the king-size mattress and gave him another taste of my deep throat head shot game before I dipped out back to the other hotel to meet up with Melanie, who was more than likely ordering room service and VIP massages on my pockets. That was the type of chick she was: a user who loved to try to get over on muthafuckas. Nevertheless, me and her had some preparing to do.

Izzi

Zaria was getting ready to ball in dangerous territory. Nardo had messed her head up so much that she was just ready to fuck him over and shit. Since I was trying to be on the come-up and he was slow-walking, I might as well join in on the scheme.

"What up, dude?" I asked Nardo when I called him. I was lying in the bed recuperating from the wild sex me and his baby momma just had. She was definitely gonna be a keeper if baby girl could keep me cumming like she had.

"Slow motion, slow motion. Now, what's up on that stripper's situation? A nigga dick is a li'l dry, and I'm not trying to head to the crib with Spice."

"Man, that broad, sac-chasin' Sara, I used to bang out said they was throwing the set. I'll go trick my cash off on her for a while, but you know she gotta pay with that ass afterwards." I got a hard-on picturing Zaria, not Sara, naked. No doubt I was trying to tap some of my new wifey when we left the club later.

"That's what's up. What time you trying to hit it up?" Nardo quizzed.

"About twelve. We gonna VIP all night, you know, so damn trying to get seated up front. You feel me?"

"Squared up. I'm about to swing by the condo and check on my spot, and I'll meet you on the block in a few. We can take separate cars just in case one of us gotsta bounce."

I set the phone down and rubbed my manhood, thinking about Zaria. She had me open, but that pregnancy predicament was not gonna work. I was trying to savage fuck the baby out of her earlier, but it was a trooper. I guess the little fetus had his protective headgear on and was not gonna go without a fight.

Anyhow, I got up and jumped in the shower to get myself together. I threw my clothes on and was out the door. I had to get to Zone 8 and hook up this spot.

Fuck Nardo and Zaria. I got money to make!

CHAPTER SEVENTEEN

Spice

"Renard! I'm so sick and tired of you completely disregarding my feelings and doing me wrong for her. I cook, clean, keep you sexually pleased, and give you access to my money. I deserve more than you allowing your baby momma to run up on me. If you don't want to answer the phone, then to hell with it and you! Yo' shit will be on the curb," I hollered onto Nardo's voice mail before hanging up and calling again.

I couldn't believe Zaria's childish, good-for-nothing begging behind was pregnant again. On top of it all, Nardo had the nerve to be mad at me because I was tired of all the over-the-top, constant drama she brought. I didn't know why she just couldn't leave him alone. The whole ordeal was taking a toll on me.

"Renard!" I screamed when he finally answered to my incessant calling. I was not giving up without a fight.

"I see you calling, but damn, I ain't interested in the shit you gotta say, Spice. Now, give a nigga some space, will ya?" Nardo fired back, not giving me a chance to vent first.

I'd been calling every minute on the minute since he dropped me and my son off, but he was probably so busy trying to chase and mend stuff with Zaria's knocked-up ass that he was forgetting about home and that I could have problems going on, too, with the crazy, twisted-up love triangle situation he caused. It was like he had a blindfold on to what was so obvious: my love and devotion.

"I need you to come home." I ignored his harsh words. "Right now!"

"Spice, you always in need. You turning into my damn baby momma with all that needy, clingy crap. We ain't got no kids, so I don't owe you nothing."

"Go to hell, Renard. I'm done! Yo' shit will be curbside," I repeated, hanging up the phone.

I picked up my car keys and got my little man in the car. We was about to take a short road trip. Bottom line, I was headed to Zaria's house. Me and her was gonna straighten this bullshit out once and for all! Tonight, Nardo would have to choose between us.

Zaria

I walked into the Doubletree and enviously looked around at all the couples that were enjoying each other's company and seeming to be overly happy. I'd never completely felt satisfied with Nardo. I loved my child's father unconditionally, but we spent so much time arguing and debating his trifling ways that we never got the chance or opportunity to enjoy each other fully. Now, here my dumb ass was with one small baby, a pregnant belly, and a heart ready to kill. The next guy to come around would hate that he crossed my path. I could see it now. My life would be a perfect sequel to *A Thin Line between Love and Hate*. I was damaged goods.

Damn that Renard!

I opened my room door and walked straight to the shower to turn it on. Before getting undressed, I stuck my head into the other room to see what my newly ordained partner in crime was up to. *This tramp*! Melanie was stretched across the bed, eating hotel food on my pockets, just as I predicted, watching syndication re-runs of *Girlfriends*.

"Hey, girlie!" Melanie greeted me as if we were best friends all over again.

"Hello." I could barely stomach the words as my skin crawled at the sight of her. "I see you been chilling."

"Yeah, I figured I deserved a treat after them hours you made me spend behind bars."

"Whatever, Melanie."

"Girl, be quiet. I can't hear my show."

Damn, I wish I could be so carefree and reckless and just up and leave this hood and all its bullshit, I thought as I went into the other room and pulled out my clothes for the night. "Will you be ready by the time I get out the shower?" I yelled out to Melanie.

"That must've been some good dick." She sucked her teeth, not even answering my question.

"How you figure I was out having sex?"

"Look who you are talking to first. Second, your hair looks like you've been broke and on the corner all day in a windstorm," she cleverly observed.

I snickered at her comment after taking a quick look in the mirror. I hadn't even noticed I was messy as hell. "Well, yeah, it was worth it, since you so nosy!"

"So, if you're pissed at Nardo, who's doing the dipping?" She rolled over, fully diverting her attention from the television. "Who blew yo' wig back?"

I'd been so caught up in the money and life without eviction notices and broke-down hoop rides that I had forgotten about having real friendships. Mel was so chill and was acting like we were back in middle school, laughing and joking about a little crush we had. The shit was mad relaxing, low key. For months Kimmie was the only person I had kicked it with about my problems, and she was a foreign chick, so she really couldn't connect to the mess I was going through. She was just faking the funk.

"Earth to Zaria . . . Hello!" Melanie screamed, bringing me out of my daydream.

"Oh, dang gee, I was just caught up in my thoughts."

"On what?"

"I would tell you something, but you might trip."

"What is it, girl? Tell me! Tell me!" Melanie sat up in the bed and started crunching on an overpriced bag of potato chips.

"All right then, but calm the hell down!"

Okay, okay, okay!" Melanie was eager for me to confide in her. "Tell me, girl. I'm listening."

"Well," I slowly started off, swallowing a lump in my throat, "me and Izzi been messing around."

"Get the fuck out of here! You mean to tell me that you're letting Nardo's right hand get all up in it?" She leaped to her feet spilling chips on the carpet. "You nuts!"

"Oh, so are you the judge-a-ho police now?"

Naw, I'm not judging you. Guess if you fuck over your best friend, then you'll fuck over your mans with his best friend."

Melanie was being sarcastic as hell, making me regret dropping my guard and telling her my damn business. But I guess I got caught up in the moment of having a "friend."

"Yeah, well, I guess I would." I rolled my eyes, annoyed that we had to keep getting back on that subject.

"So, what are we about to get into?" She sensed I was pissed. "I'm ready to hang."

"Some revenge, so dress down," I growled, walking into the bathroom and shutting the door.

I called the babysitter to check in, making sure all was well with Cidney, and then I got naked and stepped into the hot shower. The water ran down my back, and I began to feel somewhat relaxed. I meditated on everything that was going on with me. Reality hit hard. I was ashamed of myself. I'd lost control over my life. If my mother ever found out about all the things I'd done this past week and all her rules I'd broken, she'd disown me for certain.

Get it together! Get it together!

I let myself cry to get out some of my anger and frustration. The need to ball up in the corner of the shower and die was tempting, but I couldn't lose my mind just yet, I had business to take care of.

"Zaria, you all right in there?" Melanie tapped on the door, acting as if she truly gave a rat's ass about my well-being.

"Yeah, I'm cool. Give me a minute and I'll be out in a few."

As I was drying off, I began to rub my stomach. There was a little life growing inside of me, and I had the audacity to despise its very existence. Nardo had fucked me over so much that I didn't have any emotion over this pregnancy, which is supposed to be the happiest time in a woman's life. As for my daughter, I was even short-changing her. What was happening? Cidney was not close to getting the mother she deserved, and Nardo's punk ass ain't care about shit but his own self-preservation. Well, tonight I would be done with Nardo.

I turned the flat iron on high so I could freshen up my weave and began to apply lotion all over my body. I was going to tear some stuff up later, but there was no reason for me to look like a dirtball while I was in the process of doing so.

"You don't have to dress in sneakers, but don't dress like we're going to the club either," I hollered into the other room to Melanie. I was trying to go out in style.

Combing my hair, I let it fall down straight to my shoulders. Walking out into the room, I saw Melanie dressed in a pair of Luxerie denim jeans and matching T-shirt, probably from some knockoff store, and some dirty shoes. She looked so below average, but hey, I couldn't expect anything else. She was cute in her own way, I guess, but not a showstopper like me. Unfortunately, she didn't know how to keep her appearance up, or she lacked the funds to do so. Not only were her clothes subpar, she was just plain messy. Her hair was brushed back in a regular, old-school ponytail with a filthy scrunchie, and her eyebrows looked as if they belonged to the nearest beast at the local kennel.

"We have to make a stop before I get to my final destination," I informed Melanie as I finished getting dressed.

I put on a black baby doll dress that bunched up at the bottom. I had picked it up from H&M at the mall. I accessorized with silver bangles, big silver hoop earrings, and a silver necklace with a cross encrusted with diamonds. I sprayed on a little Paris Hilton and stepped in front of the mirror to make sure everything was top notch and perfect.

"Damn, Zaria, what magazine are you trying to be in?" Melanie sounded envious as she watched me like a hawk sizing up its prey.

"Don't hate. Copy if need be," I advised, laughing, but I was dead serious. "Just don't hate."

"Fuck you, Zaria." Melanie smacked her lips and pulled out her knockoff Gucci purse and put on her cheap ninety-nine-cent lip gloss and her dollar store earrings. My ex-friend had fallen off badly. Had it been any other day or any other circumstances, I wouldn't be caught dead rolling with something of that quality. After tonight, she and I were history.

CHAPTER EIGHTEEN

Zaria

I came off the Lodge Freeway onto Jefferson Avenue and popped in a mix CD I'd picked up of Ashanti. I was feeling all her tracks, especially the one called "Foolish." I noticed Melanie, who was riding shotgun, was feeling the song too. We were even singing the lines word for word.

See my days are cold without you, but I'm hurting while I'm with you.

Y'all know she really hit the nail on the head with that line.

Riding past Hart Plaza, I noticed the African World Festival was on bump. There were crowds of people everywhere, enjoying the warm night air. The more I saw cars with rims and sounds, chicks trying to floss for the dudes who were bossing, and the stores filled up with alcoholics, I got angrier and extremely bitter. These people were enjoying the world, while my life reeked of sheer nothingness. As I drove, I yearned for and could almost taste revenge for my sorrows.

I just wanna be happy.

Restaurant lots were on jump. Part of me wanted to stop and parking-lot pimp, but I had an agenda that couldn't be ignored. I was on a serious mission. Living with the fact that I hadn't had been able to hold down a decent meal in days, I changed my mind to stop. I needed some nourishment if I wanted to be at full capacity to destroy Nardo's punk ass.

I pulled into the Wendy's lot partly because I was hungry, but mainly because it was on bang. I decided a girl had to have a little fun and stress relief. My nerves were on edge, and butterflies were set in my stomach, as my plan would soon be put into complete, total effect. Any consequences that occurred after this night would have to be put in the hands of the Almighty God.

"Damn, ma, come over here for a second." A guy who was sitting in the passenger's side of an old-school Cutlass with an out-cold, purple flip-flop paint job said, "Let me speak to you."

I was not trying to pay him any attention. First, he was not the driver (I know I'm a shallow bitch, but so be it!) and second, I didn't have time for any amateur player trying to push up on me. Melanie, on the other hand, started tapping my shoulder like she was working for him.

"Hey, Zaria, he calling you!"

"Chill, Mel. I ain't deaf. Is you on his payroll or what?" I kept a straight face, walking through the door at Wendy's. Without so much as making slight eye contact, I told him, "I'm sort of in a hurry."

"I can dig it, so I'll kick it with you inside," he insisted, getting out of the car.

Damn! This is what I get for trying to come show off—a low-budget nigga trying to talk to me. Why didn't I just go through the drive-up window?

I got in line to place my food order, and out the corner of my eye, I watched him approach the door. He was tall and slender in stature. His skin was dark, rich cocoa brown in color, and the brotha rocked a pair of gold wire-framed glasses. His gear was top notch, though. Flossing a cream-and-black linen shirt, black pants, and black Cole Haan shoes, he was doing his thing. Most dudes nowadays wore iced-out chains, but this guy wore a simple gold chain with a cross pendant, a nice watch, and a platinum-and-diamond pinky ring. Observing and sizing a Negro up quick was another skill my mother had schooled me on.

Getting a closer look at the entire package when he got directly in my face, I liked what I saw. His haircut was fresh to def, and his goatee and beard had to have been lined up with a razor, because it was so crisp. His cologne undeniably had a chick like me mesmerized. I loved his scent right off rip.

"So, what's your rush, girl?" He grinned, showing his perfect white teeth, finally being in close enough range to have a personal conversation.

"Sorry, sweetie, but I have errands to run and not much time to be here parlaying and letting guys hit on me." I shot him down even though he was fine.

"Welcome to Wendy's. Can I take your order?" The cashier chewed her gum like a mule.

"Yeah, let me have two five-piece nuggets and a small Pepsi."

"Oh, I got it, girl." The mystery man pulled out his wallet—not a knot of money in a rubber band, but a wallet like a grown-ass man.

"Big spender, oooooh!" Melanie disrespectfully blurted out, trying to be all up in my mix. "If you treating like that, then you could pay for me too."

Dang, this chick was ignorant! This guy hadn't paid her any attention, so she just had to make her presence felt. He immediately gave Melanie's desperate ass a twenty and told her to order her food and keep the change if any. Then he asked me politely to step to the side and reward him with a few brief seconds of my time. Even though I had a lot on my mind, after Melanie's smart-talking ass, I felt I owed him at least that much consideration.

Dude's name was Erik, and he was from Indiana. From the way he carried himself, I knew he had manners. If it would've been any other time, I would have been all on him. I could tell he was down for some real-type cake stuff, and he obviously could tell from my demeanor what ballpark I played in—the majors!

"All right, call me sometime, girl. Okay?" He was smooth as he finished up the conversation and started to walk toward the door. "I'll be waiting."

"Thanks for the meal, sexy," Melanie flirted as the doors were shutting behind him.

Dang! She was so embarrassing. By the time we got to the car, Erik and his friend had pulled off.

I just might call him. He do look good as hell, I thought to myself as I opened the barbecue sauce and dipped my first nugget.

As I cruised up Jefferson Avenue to get to Lafayette, I finally divulged to Melanie what the plan was. Phase one, we were going to ransack Nardo's condo and completely destroy everything that was important to him. She was, of course, all for it. After a quick stop at CVS to purchase a Green Dot card that I would use later to fill up my gas tank, I put the pedal to the floor to get to Nardo's. Time was running out for my baby's daddy. With the aid of Melanie riding shotgun and Izzi down at the club, that two-timing cheater would pay!

Nardo

Bitch, shake yo' ass. It's time to throw this money! USDA's song was banging in the titty bar. Me and Izzi was in VIP, getting lap dances, both throwing back drinks like a muthafucka. I had my eye on one young thang in particular that was working the room. You could tell she was semi new to this club, because she was somewhat timid around the other regular bitches who kept griming her. Nubian Delight, as the DJ called her when she took the center stage, was a new face and a fresh new piece of pussy, so every guy wanted her. New tail, especially untainted tail, was the best tail in the stripping game.

"Let me get two bottles of Moët," I commanded the waitress.

"Anything else, honey?"

Yeah, bring me back two shots of Patrón." Izzi glanced upward as he was getting frisky with a dancer.

My boy was straight out his hookup tonight. He was tipping girls twenties and shit like they were going out of style. Me, there was no way I was tipping like that unless I was getting some serious head or a dripping wet dick. I just kicked back and enjoyed watching Izzi straight clown. For a brief moment, I let my mind drift back to who I had waiting back at home—Spice. When I left here, I was going to get me some true island banging. I was going to make up with her, but I had to make sure she was in check. I'd let her get way too far out of pocket; that was my fuck-up, but bet money you wouldn't catch me slipping twice.

"Wanna dance?" Nubian Delight licked her lips eagerly as she approached me after coming down off the stage. "I peeped you watching me."

Baby doll was a coffee brown goddess with a dime-piece centerfold body that was slamming. Her wavy, long hair made her look like a mermaid, and with firm breasts and a plump behind, her appearance was perfect. She had on a peach one-piece dress thrown over her shoulder and a matching G-string on her ass. Ol' girl looked mad sexy.

"Get on that, cuzzo, and tip the bitch good," Izzi shouted out over the loud music, not caring if he disrespected the female.

She seemed to go unfazed by his remarks, because she didn't even blink. She must've been used to that type of talk. Moving closer to me as sounds of Genuwine's song "Anxious" filled the club, she rubbed on her breasts. "If you like the dance, then maybe you'll want more of this." She seductively licked my ear as she climbed on my lap and slowly started to grind to the beat. "You know you wanna release that big monster growing in your pants. don't you?"

I liked her forward style. Her moves had me on rise and ready to take things to the next level. Unlike other dances I got, copping feels seemed to excite her even more.

"Take her freak ass into the back and show her how real Linwood boys do," Izzi flossed, handing me two hundred-dollar bills.

Ol' girl didn't even wait for me to take the money from Izzi. Instead, she snatched it out of his hands and told me to show her what he was talking about. I could tell she enjoyed the hell outta her job.

Izzi winked his eye at her, and she blew him a kiss.

Damn, she's a tramp!

As she stood up, her breasts were standing at full attention. Not bothering to cover herself while we were walking to the Black Hole, as it was nicknamed, she just smiled.

"You must don't know who you about to fuck with, li'l momma," I warned her as we got into one of the private rooms.

"A Linwood cat, I assume," my soon-to-be private dancer replied, getting smart.

"You got a lot of mouth." I barely spoke before she pushed me back on the couch.

"Yeah, I've been told that, but I know how to back up everything I say. And real talk, my mouth won't get me into no type of trouble I can't get out of." She sucked my fingers slyly, letting me know she was down for the whole nine. "Matter of fact, I'm tired of talking."

"Well, maybe you should put something in that mouth of yours."

"Yeah, you right." Nubian Delight stuck her tongue out so I could see the glowing ring that pierced the center.

"Damn, it's like that, huh?"

"Yeah, it is, daddy. There's no dry run here."

"Well, put my dick where your mouth is!" In other words, I was also tired of the talk. I wanted action.

She dropped down on her knees and started doing her thang. I knew she would be wild, but ooooh-weee she was off the hook!

Suck this big, black dick, ya nasty bitch! Suck it! Suck it!

Every time I thought the show was over, she was back on me, and I never turned down pussy or head. I had to have banged the trick three or four good times before I walked out of that private room, not even knowing her government-issued name. Despite what you heard, there is definitely sex in the champagne room, especially if enough dough is involved.

Spice

I pulled up to Zaria's little upscale suburban home and went to ring the doorbell. No one came to the door, and there was no vehicle in the driveway. Walking back to my car, I called Renard, and of course, no big surprise, there was no answer from him. I was irritated that I was forced to leave another message. It was probably the tenth or eleventh one that hour.

"I'm at Zaria's house, so I guess when you pull up, I'll see you. I'm tired of the game, Renard. This is the final play!" I hung up, pissed off.

Combing my freshly done braids, I gathered them with my hands into a ponytail. I wrapped a scarf around my head, greased up my face, and began to relax. I soon reclined my chair and turned Alicia Keys' *Songs in A Minor* on low, so as not to wake my son, who was fast asleep in the rear seat, as I meditated.

CHAPTER NINETEEN

Zaria

Nardo stayed in a quiet subdivision of condos. He often bragged that he'd been staying over there for years without incident. Not one of his well-to-do neighbors ever questioned how he dressed and drove so flossy and never seemed to go to work. I rarely visited this place. Nardo claimed this was his place of absolute solitude, where he could go to escape the drama of the streets, so we were always at my crib.

"You ain't scared, Zaria?" Melanie dumbly asked me.

"Naw, so if you are, you might want to shake the shit off. I'm here for business and business only," I let her know in no uncertain terms.

I pulled up into his attached garage. If he did come home, he'd be shocked as hell. He didn't even know that I'd had a key made a few months back, when Cidney had just been born and I ran to get Pampers in his car because he'd blocked mine in. Bet that dummy would think twice the next time he trusted some hood chick from the D.

Please, let my key still work. I pulled my spare key from my purse. Until now, I was not thinking it might not work. Nardo could have changed the locks, which would've wrecked my entire plan. I smiled when I turned it and the door opened. *Oh, yeah, he's gonna shit bricks once he finds out what I used this emergency key for.*

I walked into his bachelor pad with a plan that only a bitter baby momma could carry out. With no time to waste, I went straight into the kitchen and began to pull out all the dishes and glasses, shattering them into a million tiny pieces.

Appearing insane herself, Melanie took a butcher knife and began to spontaneously cut the electrical cords on the fridge, toaster, microwave, blender, and any other appliances in her scorned path. I snatched a gallon of milk out of the fridge, splattering it everywhere, so his entire crib would smell spoiled and just all-out stank. Turning on the water, I plugged the stainless steel sink with several dish rags, walking the fuck away with not so much as a second thought.

With total pride and no regrets in my stride, I marched into the living room and started knocking all the games, DVDs, and CDs off the entertainment center and onto the floor. The devil himself seemed to be helping me as I smashed each one. While in the process of my chaotic vindictive rampage, I called Izzi.

"Hey, girl, what's up?" he shouted into the phone.

I could barely make out his words because wherever he was at, the sounds were banging. I was jealous that my Izzi seemed not to be missing me. In the background, I could hear a DJ and a lot of people.

"Where you at?" I yelled back, hoping he'd realize I was mad that he was out having such a good damn time.

"All-Stars," Izzi respond in a suddenly quieter voice. "My bad. I was inside with all the noise. So, what's up, baby?"

"Why you all up in the strip club? My ass ain't pretty enough to look at?"

"Damn, Z! Hold the fuck on! Didn't you tell me to keep your punk-ass baby daddy occupied?" Izzi questioned me.

"Yeah, I did." I realized that I'd overreacted. "I was just saying."

"Well, that's what I'm doing. He's inside chillin'."

"Who drove?"

"We came in separate rides. I drove my drop-top. Why you ask?"

"Because I'm at his condo, so please don't let him leave until I call you again. I'm trying to finish up." I gave him an update so he could keep his game right, but I ignored his original question. I didn't want him to think I was being overly concerned about Nardo. He might have stopped helping me, and now was not the time for any distractions from the plan.

"All right. I got him in there with a girl I used to trick with a while back. He's wide open off the little ho for real. I tipped her good to come on to him, so you owe me one."

"I paid a little of that debt off earlier, but I got you later, too. By the way, what's that whore's name?"

Before Izzi could answer, I heard the sounds of leather furniture being ripped. Melanie was slicing and dicing, which geeked me up, like Ike beating Tina. I shoved Nardo's 42-inch television over, crashing it to the polished hardwood floor.

"Whoa, ya over there on some Rambo-type movement. Remind me not to fuck you over!" He paused. "But back to your question, I don't know her government name."

"What are you good for?" I chuckled in a playful tone as I smashed Nardo's custom made lamps.

"Chill, girl. Why you need to know anyway? Is she gonna be next on your list?"

"Forget it. Just keep Nardo there until further notice and away from his truck. I have to get back to business."

Melanie was angrier than I originally thought. She was cursing Nardo's very existence in life the whole time she was destroying his property. I left her beyond bitter butt to finish off the front area of the condo as I made my way upstairs with a big jug of Clorox bleach that I'd found in the laundry room.

CHAPTER TWENTY

The Connect

"What's up, Izzi?" I picked up my cell, expecting his call.

"It's slow motion this way. Out shooting moves. Have you had a chance to think on that conversation we had earlier?" He cut straight to the chase.

"I did, and a plan might can be orchestrated that will work out for the best of us." I put his wondering mind to ease. "But before we seal the deal, let's meet up in the morning and speak on everything face to face."

"Cool. Same place?"

"Nine in the morning sharp, Izzi. On the nose, and not on my people's time. We can't stay two steps ahead if we're trying to catch up."

"I got you, and I'll be there on time. Nine a.m. sharp."

"A'ight, stay up." I ended the call, ready to sit down from shooting my own moves all day.

Taking my gold Cartier wire frames off my face, I set them on the dashboard of my Lexus truck and rubbed down my beard while inhaling deeply. Though I was away from home, I wasn't on a vacation. This gritty city was far from the Miami beach I wished me and a baddie were laid up on, sipping beers. Instead, me and my homeboy rode the entire of city of Detroit; but he was now retired to the crib with his woman and kids. I was looking to set up shop the right way, then fall back and let my hands get washed cleaned.

Nardo and I had been doing business for years, almost as long as I had been connecting hustlers to quality product. He proved his loyalty to me time over and then again, which was why I allowed him to bring Izzi to the table for an introduction in the first place. The two of them were supposed to be moving as a unit, Izzi as Nardo's right-hand man, but it was clear Izzi's hand was more about the stab-and-take-down.

I saw the hunger in Izzi's eyes the very first time I shook his hand. His grip was equally strong and firm, which let me know he was the muscle of the two. I was not surprised that Izzi requested a one-on-one sit down, but that it took him as long as it did.

Nardo's way of thinking was slow and steady. He was more of a map planner. Izzi, on the other hand, was the flip side of the coin. He was a maverick and a risk taker. I believed he would take Nardo's territory with or without my backing, so I chose to fund the winning team. I was not hustling to make lifelong friends, but enemies and long paper. When you lived in a world that was governed by drugs, death, deception, and the almighty worshiped dollar, you had to take risks if you wanted to survive.

The game plan layout was lovely. Every intoxicant you could think of would be set up in what Izzi referred to as the "gutter zone." Me and my boy rode through the neighborhood like the feds. The house Izzi was proposing he transform into a trap house was located in a central spot with a lot of foot traffic, mainly represented by low-budget hookers, small-time nickel-and-dime hustlers, and a huge population of dope fiends, all of whom were symbols of income for me. Me and my ace watched sales go down all day.

I did not doubt Izzi's guarantee to quadruple the amount of money he and Nardo were bringing to the table already, but what would come of him cutting his partner out? I would be fronting way too much product for some shit to pop off then have all the risk and loss fall back on me. A man of my caliber moved at a calculated speed, however.

Swigging the last bit of beer that was left in the can, I tossed it out into the waste can a few feet away from where I was parked, while waiting on my family from Indiana to answer the phone. Unlike the way Izzi claimed loyalty to Nardo, how I connected to and related with my day ones was much different. We would make together, take together, and break bread together.

"Yo, E. What's good, my baby?" My cousin answered, glad to hear from me.

Before I hit the highway to Detroit, I'd met up with him and his brother, plus another one of our cousins. We come from a big family. I even had a few female hustlers that were a part of my bloodline. The sit-down was to discuss what my trip to the city was about and what this call would be about, if it was made. We were a family that *preyed* together.

"Nothing but good news. I got a connect with this dude who works in different factories through temp services. I just put my application in this morning, so you can make your way here to put your application in within the next week or so." Half of my story was bullshit. He knew exactly what I meant, which was that he, his brother, and our other cousin needed to be on the road headed here from Indiana tonight. It was time to put my family to work so we could all eat from what Izzi had already thrown into motion. I was not bringing them to this city to take over and monopolize his plan, but to sit on both Nardo and Izzi's turf to make sure my investment was not wasted. The only reason we would start making noise and sending gunshots into the air was if Izzi's moves started swaying left.

Leaning back in my seat, I took a few deep breaths, wishing I had a woman to accompany me into my apartment. A nightcap that ended with my penis in some pretty girl's mouth and then vagina would have been the perfect way to put me to sleep. I had a gang of hoes in Indiana, but none here in the city of Detroit on speed dial. If these niggas didn't roll as grimy as they were known to do, or if my cousins were already in town some, I would have run up in a strip club to get entertained. Every man requires a daily dosage of ass.

After I looked around for any unfamiliar cars, I climbed out and walked into my bachelor pad. It wasn't nothing much but a flat screen television, a cheap-ass living room and bedroom set I cashed out on from off West Eight Mile, some dishware for me to eat off of, and the basic necessities I needed to wash my ass. I set this crib up so I could live comfortably while I was monitoring, and I could not do that in a motel.

Plopping down on the couch, I got the Fire Stick started up so I could watch a few movies. It was not common that I closed my eyes and slept, especially in a foreign place. That was another reason why I needed a loyal-ass lady friend. Instead of watching movies and stroking my own nut up out of my dick on a rough night, I could be curled up to and deep inside of her. Every real successful player needs a chick by his side to ride with, and I was no different than the next. Even an honest living man who works a nine-to-five needs a companion to share his take-home wealth with.

My eyes might have been staring at the television screen, but my mind wandered. I was thinking about business and how I needed to level up sooner than planned. I even thought about having my family bring along a hot piece of ass for me to climb into once they arrived, but I knew none of my shorties would want to depart in the morning back to Indiana by train or bus, leaving me to tend to my business. I could not and would not allow myself to be distracted with so much of my product on the line.

I then thought about the shorty I'd met at Wendy's earlier and wished I had pressed her harder for her seven digits. Honey was fine as hell, with a banging-ass body, just the type of chick I could be cuddled up with right about now. She seemed to have that intelligent, classy look, topped off with a little gangster edge. I liked homegirl's style and was definitely hoping she'd hit me up.

Izzi

Rubbing my hands together like a greedy muthafucka does, I was feeling anxious, yet like a boss, that my plans were starting to go into play. The connect had agreed to the proposition I put before him to make more dough. I knew he wouldn't resist the temptation, but what concerned me was him being cool with me fuckin' over Nardo. I was gonna keep it about money, but he and I would be watching each other. From this point on, my movements were about to be carefully calculated, and I would be thinking things through a little more thoroughly.

Zaria would keep me grounded some because having a wifey at home that knew the rules of the dirty game I was intent on playing would help me stay focused. But with her firecracker temper, which was always out of control, I knew she was one female that would keep me knee deep in trouble. I'd already low-key flipped for her ass, but me wanting Nardo out the game completely now made me want to wife her even more. First getting the pussy was meant to be just a smack in the face to Nardo, but now I wanted his baby momma on my team full time. The main rule was broken—money over bitches. Yeah, that was done. Me and Zaria was getting it in!

After hanging up from Zaria, I made another call while waiting on Nardo to come out of the Black Hole, where I knew my girl had him going. See, I'd slipped a special pill in his drink for extra measure so his game would be a little off point. Nardo didn't do drugs, so he would be way off his square. First highs often did that to you.

I heard a loud engine that I knew wasn't a car and looked up to see a tow truck pulling into the parking lot.

"Shorty is crazy as hell," I murmured to myself about Zaria, then ran back into the club to stall Nardo.

Her deck of cards is definitely missing a few Spades.

Zaria

"I told Nardo to stop toying with my heart. I begged him to either love me or let me be," I spoke out loud to no one in the room, and then started having a full conversation with myself. "He made you do this crazy shit, Zaria. It is all his fault his apartment will be ransacked, his prize possessions will be ruined, and the precious vehicle he cherishes so much will need a new paint job. For him hurting your daughter, he deserves all of this and more."

With my feet kicked up and crossed, I was in Nardo's bed, laid back on his fluffy pillows, fiddling with my cell phone. My mind was racing as I tried figuring out what more devious acts I could pull off. No longer did I want us to work it out. I was trying to send this nigga to the grave from a heartache for breaking mine.

My cell phone rang and snatched me out of my thoughts. It was the driver at Nu Wave Towing.

"Hello," I answered, nervous that he was about to say he could not get the car.

"Yes, ma'am. Can you confirm the address I'm supposed to deliver the car to?"

"Do you have it already?" I answered a question with a question, needing to know his answer first.

"Yeah, so—"

I cut him off. The world *yes* was all I wanted to hear. After giving him Nardo's address, which he thought was mine, we hung up, and I sat up to take a few deep breaths. I'd called the towing company with Nardo's license plate number and a fabricated story. Since they were well known in and around metro-Detroit for being a shady renegade towing company that stayed under investigation for illegal operations, I knew I would not have to put much into the story or even be on site for them to snatch up the vehicle. All they cared about was that cash, and I gave them a Green Dot Visa card that went through for a five hundred-dollar transaction.

I told them I was a dancer at the strip club and was far too intoxicated to drive home and didn't want to risk getting pulled over by the police. I told them I was getting into a cab but to drop it off at my house and I would be there with a cash tip. Sticking to their no-questions-asked tactics, I was now on a time clock to tear some more shit up.

Leaping up from the bed I once use to lay in with Nardo, I started pulling all of his clothing out of the dresser drawers and tossing it around the room. One quick run to the bathroom cabinet and I was equipped with gloves and bleach to ruin all of his belongings. I walked around his room, whistling and tossing bleach carelessly. I slung so much onto his clothes, shoes, bed, carpet, and walls that I started feeling nauseated from the overpowering smell. I ended up having to open the window for a fresh breeze and putting my shirt over my nose and mouth to look for the spare key to Nardo's whip. My eyes took the biggest hit and were stinging red by the time I was done.

I should drive that car straight into the Detroit River. I was letting my thoughts get carried away.

I could hear Melanie still smashing various items downstairs. At this point, I was glad I had help accomplishing my goal. Project Fuck Nardo was going better and smoother than I thought it would. All I wanted was his love and truth, but he only gave me lies.

With great contempt, I made my way into his walk-in closet and started cutting up all his shirts and jeans. I made sure every single thing that was hanging up was destroyed and he'd have to start over from scratch to jump fresh again. I slashed, sliced, and cut until my fingers grew tired and started aching; then I took a break and started cutting up all his shoes. Nardo had a fetish for sneakers, so I knew this revenge would hit his heart hard. Anything that meant something to Nardo, I wanted it ripped from him.

Forced to slow down my crazed rage, I saw some notebook paper folded up on the floor that must have fallen from one of the shoe boxes. It looked like a letter. When I knelt down to pick it up to see, I ended up finding the box it fell out from, which was really a treasure box of trick shit. The Nike shoe box was full of pictures, more letters, and bills of money.

I hurried up and found an empty spot on the floor to sit, then started counting all the bills I was about to bag. I didn't want to take them all, but enough to feel whole. The money was the most important thing— until I saw some pictures of ol' girl downstairs.

Nardo

I saw Izzi frantically rushing back into the club like it was some shit popping off outside, but my limbs and brain were not working together for me to jump up for possible action. Tonight's ingestion of alcohol and marijuana had me weirdly feeling like a rookie. My buzz did not feel normal, though I had guzzled a ton of shots and drinks.

"Where did you disappear to, dude?" My question was slurred as Izzi finally approached the table.

I was not sure if it was me or not because of the buzz that had control of my body, but I swore that I saw Izzi's eyes move upward like he was trying to think of a story to tell. Me and his ass had been running as boys for so long that I knew quirks about him that he probably did not know about himself.

"You know me, my dude. I was outside tricking off some cash with one of these strippers. Shorty gave me some mad ass skull for a fifty." He was trying to sell me his tale.

I couldn't even calculate really what bag he was coming out of because I was feeling strangely buzzed. The several drinks I'd downed had taken a serious toll on a guy. "Was she tight, man?"

"Yeah, Nardo, her head game was on point. The bitch even swallowed. How was ol' girl in the back?"

"I wouldn't mind getting up in that again."

"Well, who said you had to stop?" the young dancer said, coming up behind me.

I couldn't believe all this touchy-feely stuff was going on. Usually that was not allowed. "Damn, is it like that?"

"Yeah, and maybe it can be with you and your boy." She sized Izzi up.

I was not usually down for that gang-bang mess, but I was not myself. I was fucked up, and her tight pussy was just that good that I wanted seconds on it.

"Well, get yo' hot box back to that private room," Izzi demanded, smacking her ass, still looking frantic as he kept turning back toward the entrance.

I had to remember to check him later. He seriously had to calm down with all that rough moving if we were gonna continue being partners. But for now, I just made my way back down the hallway as my dick rose to the thought of beating Nubian Delight's guts again.

CHAPTER TWENTY-ONE

Zaria

The air within Nardo's room and closet was still, stale, and starting to suffocate me. The walk-in closet all of a sudden didn't feel so big anymore as the walls were closing in. It felt like I was having an anxiety attack as my eyes scanned the floor, looking at all the freak-nasty pictures of various women he had put before me while I was busy being loyal to him and our relationship. My heart was pounding, my chest felt heavy, and my breathing was in pants. Feeling queasy like I was about to pass out from the nausea, I knelt down and picked up a few of the pictures and actually did spit up in my mouth.

The pictures were of Melanie in a bunch of different kinky positions, looking like a bootleg ghetto version of a Playboy bunny playing dress up. There were even some pictures of her sucking Renard's dick and of him actually penetrating her. Although I knew they'd slept around, I hadn't wanted the visuals embedded in my head.

"Ugh, I can't believe he actually has evidence of himself running up in this ran-through mule." I stared at her repulsive-looking, stretched-out vagina like I was into girls. I couldn't help but stare and wonder why Nardo would continuously cheat with someone beneath me. Nothing about Melanie was sexy. Hell, it looked like she was the one who'd popped a baby out of her coochie and not me. I was not even sure if Kegel exercises could help her bounce back.

"Don't get caught up on this shit, Zaria," I spoke out loud to myself, trying not to get distracted or sidetracked by the pictures. Dropping them to the floor, I kicked the box they had fallen out of out and got ready to go back into a full-blown tyrant until I saw some folded sheets of paper underneath the box. As soon as I opened it up, I knew the letter was from Melanie too. I know her handwriting from when we used to be friends writing letters back and forth to one another.

Sliding down to the floor and sitting Indian style, I clutched the letter as my eyes read the words Melanie had written:

Nardo, you know I don't have nothing but love for you. I would do anything for you, but you keep hurting me. I can't believe you would sleep with my girl. She ain't right for you, but I am. Trust me, she ain't gonna do shit but drag you down and mess over you. Zaria ain't nothing more than an opportunist and a gold digger that is looking for a meal ticket, but my love is real. I think you know that, and that's why you come and go like you do.

I guess I could count myself lucky that at least you come home to me too. The girls I call friends, they think I'm dumb for letting you have your cake and eat it too, but I don't care. If I can't have all of you, at least I can have some of you. And I know there's a reason you can't stop selling me a dream. I know you, Nardo . . . before the money, cars, and fame you have in the hood. I know how you'll make good on your word. I used to hear you tell me you'd be the boss every single day, and you did it. So, I know you'll one day make good on your word and be with me.

Every time you're in this pussy, I know it's bringing you closer back to me and tearing you away from Zaria. I know all the stuff you tell me about you not really wanting to be with her is real. I know her ass can't cook, stays in your pockets, and be bitching all the time. You wouldn't even had to have bought me a house because I keeps a Section 8 voucher on deck. I can add to your worth because I'm not coming for nothing but your heart, baby. What other bitch would've taken all that you've done and still do all that I do for you?

Zaria's probably sitting at home thinking that bastard baby mistake she carried in her sperm-polluted womb is gonna make you two a family, but she don't know that our baby is gonna bring me and you together.

I could not keep reading the letter. Not after reading her last written line. I let the pieces of paper slip from my fingers and fall to the floor.

"That stankin' ho." I staggered to my feet, blind with rage and anger. "That trick-ass slut!"

Fuck all truces, me and this female were getting ready to throw blows. I fumed out of control as I paced the floor with streams of tears flowing down from my already burning eyes. I couldn't stop thinking about Melanie probably still having his seed inside of her. Especially since she mentioned Cidney. Make no mistake about it, I wanted Melanie's head on the floor and for me to be the person to cut it off. Her being dead was the only way I could see her never being a factor in my life again. I had come too far not to want absolute revenge.

Darting over to Nardo's bedside, I fell to my knees and went straight to the lock box I knew he kept underneath it. I was determined to get satisfaction.

"What you tearing up in here, girl?" Melanie creeped into Nardo's bedroom as I started fumbling in the nightstand drawer for the key to the box.

"Melanie, don't say shit to me, ho." I was blunt and cold with my response.

"Whoa!" Melanie was thrown off by my response. "What the fuck is your problem now? Are you a manic depressive or a schizophrenic person? Why do you keep having highs and lows?" She thought she was being funny.

"You ain't shit but a little dirty wannabe-me," I shouted furiously, finally finding the key that could unlock the box where Nardo's pistol was hidden.

Melanie sighed. "A dirty wannabe-you? Um, who are you again? Why do you keep wanting to overplay your position like I don't know what position it is you really have with Nardo? I am so tired of you coming for me."

"And? So? What are you going to do about it?" I questioned her like I was ready to attack.

"Once again, you are on some nutty bullshit that I cannot vibe with or understand. I tried to be cool with you for the sake of getting back at a nigga who has done us both wrong, but forget about making amends with you or taking the fall with you. You want to keep threatening me like I don't have free will, bitch? You want to know what I'm going to do about you it? Call Nardo and tell him what is up and who threw this whole plan together, so he'll know exactly how your petty ass is stitched together. How about that?"

I went from smirking to grinning. My cheeks were actually aching from smiling so hard after Melanie's rant. She was not scaring me; she was actually adding fuel to the fire.

"You're going to call who? And tell him what? I bet you will not."

Without thinking about the consequences, or even so much as a second thought, I grabbed the pistol from its resting place then jumped up and knocked Melanie upside her watermelon-shaped head. Big shit-talking Mel didn't expect me to actually pistol whip her, and she fell to the floor. As on cue, I started kicking the brakes off the tramp and literally trying to stomp any thought of my baby daddy from her distorted-thinking brain.

Blood was gushing from the open wound on the left side of her skull and trickling out her nostril, but intent on my mission, I kept on stomping. I was paying close attention to her stomach area and that rotten, trouble-making baby her letter claimed she was carrying.

"I can't hear you, ho!" I shouted down into Melanie's face then spat on her. "Instead of giving me that long-ass speech, you should have been bracing yourself for that mighty blow that came your way. You still haven't learned the game, even after I snuck you and took Nardo from you all those years ago. Keep yo' guards up around me."

Squirming around the floor in agony, she kept trying to ball herself up in the fetal position. I took that to mean she really was pregnant and trying to protect her unborn child. That was when I swiftly kicked her in the stomach with all my strength to finish whatever job I started.

"Yeah, bitch. I'm the only one that's gonna have a kid with Nardo. Cidney does not need a little brother or sister," I taunted her, though she didn't whimper, cry out, or squirm around the floor with painful moans. Melanie was out cold, with a puddle of blood underneath her lower back and booty.

"I dare you to get up and talk shit after that beatdown," I mocked her, wishing she actually would get up so I could let out frustration on her.

I stepped over Melanie's body and ran toward the window when I heard the tow truck outside. I got there right when he was letting Nardo's truck down off the flatbed. My adrenaline was rushing like I'd experienced back to back orgasms. I had to move quickly but cautiously. I snatched the spare set of keys Nardo kept on the dresser and let Melanie bleed out on his floor so I could finish carrying out my plan. I was on a roll, too afraid to slow down.

I trotted down the stairs and opened the garage, then reversed my rental out onto the street and pulled Nardo's truck into its normal spot. I ended up giving the tow truck guy a hundred-dollar tip for him being so quick and convenient. I wanted him to remember me yet have a reason to forget me if someone asked him if he picked up a vehicle matching Nardo's from the club.

Once my tracks were covered with him, I nonchalantly strolled back into the house like Melanie wasn't upstairs passed out and I wasn't trespassing. I was out of my mind but in full control. Moving throughout Nardo's condo, I surveyed the destruction Melanie had caused before I dismantled her.

"Good job, Mel," I gave her praise, though I knew she couldn't hear me. "But if you up off that floor, round two." I climbed the stairs.

When I bent the corner, I was strangely amused to find Melanie fidgeting around. She wasn't making a lot of movement, but some was too much. I approached her body, and her eyes slightly opened, seeming to beg for mercy.

"Shhh, take it like a woman." I was ruthless, letting her know I was not about to show her a pint of pity. Picking up one of Nardo's old shopping bags, I lifted her head up and placed the plastic bag over it. She tried reaching her hands up to snatch it off but was too weak and ended up giving up. After gathering the ends and tying them into a tight double knot, I stood victoriously, with blood on my hands, and watched the bag go in and out as my once-best-friend-in-the-world struggled to breathe.

It was obvious that I'd lost my mind as I calmly finished destroying the rest of the room as a person lay there fighting for her life. The game plan had changed drastically. I was now gonna leave Mel's ass there dying, and she could take the rap for this bullshit when Nardo found her.

"You big dummy," I addressed a dying Melanie. "Did you really think my baby daddy was going to make you wifey? I know you couldn't have thought that, but then again, you always did overplay your pussy. I can't believe I wasted money getting your crappy ass out of jail," I ranted as I worked. I was feeding off her weakness.

My long weave, courtesy of Sue Lee, was starting to tangle, and my clothes looked a hot fire mess. I took notice of it as I pranced back and forth, seeing my reflection in the mirror.

"Fuck seven years of bad luck." I shrugged.

My cell phone's ringtone filled the air. As I was stepping over Mel to get to my ringing phone, somehow she must've been touched by an angel, because she found the inner strength to grab my ankle, causing me to stumble and fall. I was now face-to-face with Melanie. Through the sweaty, blood-filled plastic bag, I could see her desperate expression watching me, begging me to live.

I didn't think twice about my next actions. This trick had sucked my baby daddy's dick for the last time. It was my only alternative, and I took it. My manicured hands were shaking uncontrollably as I gripped Melanie tightly by the throat. She once again tried to struggle, but that attempt was soon cut short. After squeezing and squeezing and freaking squeezing until the plastic stopped moving and it was plastered to her face like a Halloween mask, indicating that she'd stopped breathing, I started to panic.

"Oh my God!" I shrieked out. "What did you do, Zaria? What are you going to do to fix this?" I questioned myself. Nervously leaping to my feet, I started shaking violently.

My cell phone's ringtone filled the air again. It was Izzi calling.

"Baby! Oh, shit, help!" I begged Izzi.

"What the fuck is going on?"

"I can't talk," I said, stuttering. "But I fucked up big time. I really went too far."

"Zaria, slow the fuck down and tell me what the hell is the matter?" he begged.

"Izzi, help me," I whimpered, coming to the awful realization that I was now a murderer. "Please."

"Zaria, listen to me," he demanded. "I don't know what you have done, but get the hell from in his crib and go home. I know you know Nardo's truck got towed, and I know you know we on our way out the club and that nigga is about to nut up. Go home, and I will meet you there as soon as I can."

"O . . . o . . . okay," I stuttered. Hyperventilating, I finally made my words form sentences. I ain't gonna front; I was petrified. My adrenaline was pumped up again. I was shook. "I need a little more time to finish."

"Time is up, Zaria," Izzi warned loudly.

Hanging up from Izzi, I gathered my thoughts together. I know I was not thinking clearly, but I dumbly decided to take Melanie with me until I could figure out what to do next. I clutched her arms together and dragged her out of the room. This chick was mad heavy. When I finally got her in the hallway, I was completely out of breath. Exhausted from the weight of her lifeless body, I gave her one good, hard kick in the ribs at the top edge of the stairs. Tumbling like an old rag doll, her battered torso hit the bottom landing face first, knocking out her two front teeth.

Sweat was pouring down in my eyes as I dragged her into the garage and up into the truck's rear hatch by her arms, probably ripping them out of the sockets, judging from the bone-snapping noises I was hearing. Swiftly, I ran back inside to remove any items from Nardo's house I might have left that would implicate me in this sordid mess, and then I went back in the garage.

Concealing my victim's body with the aid of an old oil-stained blanket, I was set to take off. I hit the garage door switch, cautiously peeking out. When I made sure the coast was clear, I turned the water hose on, washed my hands, then drank a small amount like a tiny child on a scorching hot summer day. Collecting my weave into a nappy ponytail and out of my face, I started Nardo's truck and slowly backed out.

As I sped up Jefferson Avenue to get home and meet Izzi, I looked over my shoulder toward the rear of the vehicle and started violently shaking all over again. It takes a different type of bitch to ride out with a corpse.

Nardo

That bitch was truly official. It slapped and was turned up fa sho'. I'd have to visit All-Stars more frequently for that head game she gave a brotha. "That was tight," I boasted to Izzi as we walked out the door of the still-crowed club.

"Yeah, man, homegirl was bad, wasn't she?" he agreed and grabbed his nuts.

"Where the fuck is my truck?" I fumed, realizing my ride was not where I'd left it. "What the fuck!"

"Man, you sure you parked it there?" Izzi dumbly questioned. "Maybe yo' cheap ass should've got valet."

"Yeah, dude, I'm sure, and now it's not here." I ran from one side of the parking lot to the next. "Somebody done took my shit. When I find out who stole my new truck, they gonna pay with they life!"

Finally, when I calmed down, I opened my cell to call the police and report my ride stolen. I noticed Spice had called more than a dozen times and left several messages, warning that she was waiting on Zaria to come home and had intentions of whooping her ass. Damn! I couldn't even take the time to call the police and make the report because I had to get to Spice before Zaria finally got home for the night and the real pandemonium started. I didn't need any more trouble for the evening.

"Izzi, Spice is over at Zaria's. Do me a solid and swing me by there. Them two chicks about to wild out!"

"Naw, dude, I wanna work with ya, but I ain't gonna be able to do it. I'm not going to be part of your circus of hoes. You on yo' own with that one, playboy." He nodded as he flipped open his phone, getting in his car.

"Nigga, did you hear me? I said I need to go by Zaria's, and you punkin' up on me? Now, come on; let's roll! I ain't gonna ask you no more."

"Man, fuck you, nigga! I ain't yo' damn flunkey! I've been banging that kitty cat anyway, and it's about damn time you found out. Now, you wanna go to Zaria's house, that's on you, but I ain't helping you do a muthafuckin' thing, so charge it to the game!"

"What you say, bitch?" I lunged at him.

"You heard me, dude!" Izzi grimed me, not moving an inch.

"Dawg, suck my dick!" I grabbed my nuts, spitting onto the ground.

"Naw guy, Zaria got this dick right here covered!" Izzi proclaimed, starting his engine and pulling off into traffic.

I couldn't move fast enough. I must've been hearing things. I replayed the conversation that had just taken place. I was still a little drunk, and my supposed-to-be homeboy had thrown me off my square, talking about he was banging my baby moms. They were both officially on my list.

Calling a cab first to get to Zaria's, then the police, I anxiously waited, pacing the club's parking lot with intense anger as several of the valet attendants looked on with a "so what your truck is missing?" attitude.

CHAPTER TWENTY-TWO

The Ultimate Revenge

Izzi

I'd kept pressing the REDIAL button over and over, trying to get through to Zaria. I was trying to plan for us to meet up at the hotel afterward. After all that had unfolded tonight, a new game plan was needed to go forward.

Why in the hell isn't she answering the phone? I hoped she wasn't going at it with Spice. Nardo's flock was all out of line. I didn't know the exact details of what went on at Nardo's condo or what she'd done, but I knew a lot of truths were about to hit the fan. I'd already brazenly snitched to Nardo about me and Zaria's secret relationship, and I already knew he was gonna try coming at me hard behind having a scarred ego. I was ready to take him out, though. Nardo ain't never been a real street nigga like he proclaimed to be.

Spice

I had been camped out in front of Zaria's house for hours. I'd even gotten out and walked around her house and looked through the windows. I hated her to my core, but I wanted to see what she was living like. I wanted to see what drew Nardo over here when he'd go against my wishes to visit. I kept thinking he was going to pull up and I was going to catch the two of them fucking around, especially since he hadn't answered the hundred or so calls I'd placed to his phone, but there hadn't been any movement.

"Mommy, the battery is red," my son whined from the back seat.

"Give it here and I'll charge it for a little bit and give it back. You can rest your eyes for a bit." I knew he was antsy from having to sit still. As soon as I looked up from plugging the tablet in, I saw Nardo's truck coming up the street and pissed in my panties.

I knew I should've listened to my daddy about your trifling ass. My eyes filled with tears and as my finger glided up and down the blade I was holding in my hand.

As the truck passed by, I looked up and saw Zaria driving it.

"What the hell is she doing driving my man's shit? Matter of fact, that's my truck as much as I've paid for it." I climbed out my car, ready to find out. "I'll be right back, baby. Stay here," I told my son then slammed my car door.

Zaria was caught up in her own world until I cut her off in mid-step.

Zaria

Once I turned onto my street, I let out the biggest sigh of my life, thankful that I was about to be at home without getting pulled over by the police. I was still paranoid and confused about what I'd done. I couldn't stop glancing over my shoulder at Melanie's wrapped-up corpse. I knew my love for Nardo ran deep, but the emotions had literally driven me crazy. I'd literally taken a life. After parking Nardo's truck a few houses down from mine, I hopped out and started rushing to my door. I was so preoccupied with my thoughts that I didn't even notice I was being watched or walked up on.

"You've got to be out of your muthafuckin' mind!" I yelled in amazement at my baby daddy's li'l island monkey. "What in the hell are you doing at my spot? Did you come here for another beatdown?" I was still frantic and in another head space over murdering Nardo's other play-toy.

"I didn't come here to play with you, Zaria." Spice exposed the knife she was holding behind her back and wildly waved it at me.

I started laughing erratically. "Girl, bye! You better make sure you kill me since you done pulled that little piece of bullshit out." I taunted her. "I ain't never let a bitch threaten me and get away with it!" I screamed and braced myself for a fight.

She waved her knife at me again, but closer to my face. I didn't let her arm get all the way back down or in another full motion before grabbing her wrist. I then started twisting and yanking it as hard as I could till the knife fell from her hand.

"Oh, hell naw, you should've definitely stayed in the burbs with yo' weak ass." I grabbed the knife and put it to work. I first cut her across the left side of her face. Then, I lost control and started slicing her entire face up. The same feeling that came over me when I killed Melanie had slipped inside of my spirt again. It felt like I was possessed and having an out-of-body experience. "I told you to leave me alone. I told you to leave my family alone. I fucking warned your dumb ass not to come for me."

I thought about all the nights I'd laid up lonely while Nardo laid up with her.

Izzi

I slammed on my brakes and burned rubber in the middle of Zaria's block when I saw the drama that was unfolding. It was sheer anarchy and had me stuck still. Zaria was like a savage as she slit ol' girl all across the face. I thought she was gonna fuck around and gut her, until she dropped the knife and started beating Spice's ass. I'd never seen a chick act as deranged as Zaria was acting. Her hair was all over her head, her jaws were clenched tightly with determination, and her eyes looked like she was possessed by the devil. I knew Nardo had fucked her heart up, but I had no idea he'd fucked up her mind too. It wasn't until a bright pair of headlights flashed into my face that I came out of the trance I was in.

Oh shit, let me get this girl. I jumped out of the car to disarm Zaria.

"Oh, hell naw! What the fuck is going on? Spice? Oh my God! What happened? Baby, are you okay?" I heard Nardo's yelling turn from shock to pure fear.

I turned around to see him leaping from the back seat.

Zaria

"Oh, no the fuck you didn't just scream for your precious Spice. Are you blind or something? You do see where she's laid out at, right? My fucking house. Our daughter's fucking house, shall I be all the way politically correct." My heart was racing, and I was out of breath. "You got some nerve coming to her defense," I shrieked out as I let Spice, who was begging for her life, fall to the grass. "First she can shoot my car, and now this? I'm the one constantly being disrespected—by you and her."

"I *been* told you our relationship was over, Zaria, so please quit playing that victim role you love playing so much. Ain't no bitch that's fucking my homeboy a muthafuckin' victim. Real talk. Yup, the cat is out of the bag on that one. You ain't shit, and you ain't never gonna be shit." Nardo was coming toward me, fists clenched. "Now I'm about to teach you a real lesson about what disrespect really is."

"Hold up, guy! I'll put a bullet in that ass before you put a hand on her." Izzi stepped out of the shadows, making his presence known. "You better slow yo' roll."

Chuckling like he was purely amused, Nardo looked between me and Izzi like we were ghosts. "This bullshit must be a joke. Are you serious, dog?" Nardo questioned Izzi as he started walking up on me again.

"Try me. You already know I gets down," Izzi pledged.

"I can't believe I was down for you, and all this time you were running around with skeezers, getting every pussy in the world to carry your little punk children. I hope you die in your sleep, Nardo!" I shouted.

"You think I wanted kids by your trifling, stank ass? Hell to the fuck no! You didn't amount to anything before Cidney, and you ain't gonna amount to nothing never. You always gonna be a gutter rat trying to be on the come-up," he predicted before getting down on his knees at Spice's side and opening his cell up to call for help. "Go over there and suck my boy's dick like you been doing. Maybe he still wants yo' messy ass."

I looked Izzi directly into his eyes and shook my head in disbelief that he'd told Nardo about our special secret encounters. *How could you do that to me?* I puzzled as the dampness of the night surrounded me. Not a single breeze was in the air as I stood in the middle of my front lawn with my life in a complete shambles and a bloody steak knife down at my side.

All my nine-to-five nosy neighbors, who had grown to love me and my baby daughter, were all in bathrobes, standing on their porches, passing judgment on me. A small child, who appeared to be Spice's son, was banging on her car window, trying to get out and probably kick me in the leg for hurting his mother. Even the stray cat I used to give a bowl of milk to every morning walked past me, turning up his nose. And worst of all in my real-life nightmare was that Nardo's truck, which was housing Melanie's dead body, was parked just a few short yards away, waiting for someone to look in the back and discover I was a murderer. I didn't want to go on, yet I'd gone too far to turn back.

"What's next?" I lifted my head, asking God, knowing He had finally given me more than I could stand. It was then that I realized the fairytale I'd been living in my head was exactly that—a fairytale. My baby daddy was never gonna respect me or be loyal to me.

Out of nowhere, I dashed to Izzi's still-running car with revenge fueling my rampage. Hopping into his ride, I threw the gear into drive and slammed down on the gas pedal. As the automobile quickly accelerated, jumping the curb, Izzi was smart enough to get the fuck out of my way by diving into the thick row of bushes and taking cover. But Nardo, the source of all my problems, was not that fast-thinking or wise. Frozen stiff, he was dead in my path, eyes cocked wide open like a deer trapped in headlights.

"I hate you, Renard!" I relived flashbacks of all the heartache, resentment, and drama he'd taken me through as I gripped the steering wheel and pressed my foot down on the gas pedal. "I hate you. I hate you. I hate you." It felt my chest tightening as the anxiety ate me up. I couldn't see straight. I felt enraged! My heart was racing, and my veins were filled with vengeance as I rapidly increased speed toward my child's father and made contact with his body. I didn't see him helplessly soar up in the air, but I sure as hell felt him come forcefully down. Nardo's muscular frame came crashing down on top of the car's hood, making a gigantic dent when he landed.

The heavy impact of him hitting Izzi's car made me feel powerful. I'd spent too many years at his mercy. I couldn't stop laughing as I heard him crying out in pain. I felt like he deserved it. I didn't pity him.

"You're lucky I didn't kill you and that you can still fight for your life, with yo' dumb ass," I coldly shouted, then callously slammed on the brake and knocked his cheating ass onto the concrete pavement. "Matter of fact, now y'all can love up on one another in rehabilitation." I slammed on the gas pedal again, this time pulling off and over his tatted-up leg at the same time. "Bye, Renard." I had the last word, laugh, and vengeance.

"Damn. I done fucked up," I said, regretfully realizing what I'd done as I looked in the rearview mirror at the chaos in front of my house.

Oh, well! I did what I had to do. It couldn't be helped. After all, I am a woman scorned.

Now, ready or not, I was about to move on and start a new chapter in my life. There would be no more VIP treatment, no more shopping sprees, no more hair appointments, and no more pedicures at Kimmie's. No more would I be known as Zaria, the number one, top-notch bitch in Detroit. I had a new title to live up to. I would now be known as Zaria, the bitter baby momma on the run.

As I was driving and coming to grips with what I had to do, my maternal instinct kicked in. Confidently, I opened my cell to call the babysitter, informing her I was on the way to pick up my innocent baby girl Cidney, so she should have her ready.

Started from the bottom now we're here.

Started from the bottom now we're here.

My ringtone went off. I powered off my phone. I knew Izzi wasn't gonna stop calling. Wiping the multitude of tears from my eyes, I felt messed up that I couldn't talk to the one person who had been down with me, but I couldn't take the risk of answering. I didn't know if he was hemmed up, or if it was even him on the line. So much had gone down in front of my house with my neighbors watching that I was sure the police already knew my name.

I started panicking and shaking when I heard their sirens off in the distance. I didn't know if they were coming for me or not, but I rubbed my belly and took off. I was officially a pregnant chick on the run because I refused to have me and Renard's second baby in a jail cell.